The Well

by Marie Sexton

COPYRIGHT

For Karen, who tried very hard to make me believe in purple worbles, possessed laundry rooms, and haunted high schools. You were always my favorite cousin, no matter what I said when I was eight.

Several people helped me with details of this book. I want to thank professional paranormal investigator KJ McCormick for graciously answering my series of five-part essay questions. Thank you to my almost-sister-in-law Justine for hooking me up (so to speak) with KJ. Also, thank you to Jillian Stein and Virginia Hobbs for their suggestions. Virginia especially gave me some great stuff to work with. Virginia, I apologize for leaving in the Steelers reference, but I changed the name of the town just for you.

CHAPTER 1

Twelve Years Ago

"Don't be such a chicken, Haven!"

Not for the first time in his seventeen years, Haven wished he had a dollar for every time his cousin Elise had said those words to him. Ever since they were kids, she'd used that little phrase to goad him into all kinds of stupid things. But having a séance in an abandoned house everybody knew was haunted?

That was an all-new level of crazy.

"I'm not chicken," Haven told her, hoping he sounded more confident than he felt. "I just don't want to get arrested for trespassing."

He glanced over at Linsey for support. Linsey was Elise's sister, younger by three years. The girls shared the same full lips and perfect cheekbones, but where Linsey's hair was light brown, Elise's was almost black. Haven was their first cousin, midway between them in age, and felt like an ugly duckling next to them. Sure, he shared Elise's dark hair and Linsey's hazel eyes, but features that appeared striking on his female cousins felt boring and unremarkable on him. Sometimes he couldn't believe they were related at all.

Luckily, Linsey backed him up. "Haven's right. It's a bad idea."

They were at the diner on Main Street in their hometown of Hobbsburg, Pennsylvania, sipping pop while they waited for their hamburgers to arrive. Other teenagers filled the booths around them. Outside, the early August day promised a hot, sticky evening. It was one of those times when it felt like summer vacation could go on forever, even though school would start in less than a month.

Elise sighed in exasperation. "What's wrong with you guys? You have no sense of adventure."

Haven shook his head, trying not to laugh. He and Linsey had both grown up hearing Elise's wild tales and being subjected to her strange pranks. They knew her well enough to predict she'd spend the entire night trying to scare the crap out of them.

"Forget it," Linsey said. "Mom and Dad would freak."

"Mom and Dad never have to know," Elise argued. "We'll tell them we're camping out. Then, instead of going into the woods, we'll go to the old Gustafson house instead."

Linsey and Haven exchanged another glance, weighing their options. Elise was stubborn as hell. Once she latched onto an idea, it was almost impossible to talk her out of it. It was a no-win situation. They could give in now, or they could argue about it, only to give in later.

"Come on," Elise prodded, sensing their hesitation. She leaned her elbows on the table, closing the distance between her and her sister. She lowered her voice to a suggestive whisper. "Craig can come too. You guys will get to spend the whole night together."

Linsey's cheeks turned red, but Haven knew she was wavering. He had no idea whether she and her boyfriend Craig had gone all the way yet, but it looked like getting a chance to share a sleeping bag with him was enough to overcome her reluctance.

"No way," Haven said to Elise. "That means Craig and Linsey go off by themselves to make out, and I'm stuck with you trying to scare me to death all damn night."

2

Elise grinned at him, and he had a feeling she'd already anticipated this moment.

"The Hunter twins are coming too."

Haven sat back in the red vinyl booth, his protests forgotten. That changed everything. He'd been prepared to dig in his heels, but he hadn't anticipated this.

Jordan and Pierce Hunter had moved to Hobbsburg from Ohio two years earlier. For the past few months, Jordan had been like a puppy at Elise's heels, doing everything he could to get her attention. He was infatuated with her, so it wasn't surprising he'd already agreed to her crazy plan.

If Jordan came along, of course his brother Pierce would too. And if following Elise into a haunted house meant Haven had a chance to spend an entire evening with Pierce...

Well, whatever Elise had planned couldn't be all that bad, could it?

Two nights later, Haven found himself in the back seat of Jordan and Pierce's car, his stomach a knot of nervous excitement as they bounced down a washboard dirt road toward a house everybody knew was haunted. Haven's new glasses slid down his nose every time the car hit a bump. He'd already pushed them back into place a dozen times.

Jordan was driving. Haven noticed him checking the rearview mirror every few seconds. At first, he assumed Jordan only wanted to check his perfectly styled hair. Then he realized Jordan was verifying that Elise, Linsey, and Linsey's boyfriend Craig were still behind them in Craig's car. Jordan's obsession with Elise definitely hadn't waned any.

Pierce, who was often as scruffy as his brother was well-groomed, turned partway around in his seat to smile at Haven. "Where's your book? I hardly ever see you without one."

His tone was friendly enough, but Haven's cheeks began to burn just the same. "I figured it'd be too dark to read." He decided not to mention that he had one stuffed in his bag, just in case. He had a feeling Pierce wouldn't have laughed, but Jordan might have.

"Do you think we'll really see a ghost?" Pierce asked.

Haven laughed, shaking his head. "There's no such thing as ghosts."

The Gustafson property lay tucked into a secluded clearing about two miles out of town. Several NO TRESPASSING signs punctuated the dirt road, which finally ended at a makeshift gate. It was only a chain strung across the trail, but between it and the thick trees, it was impossible to drive any farther. Jordan and Craig pulled their cars into the shade of the trees and began unloading their gear. They'd have to hike the last half mile.

They began their walk, arms full of sleeping bags, duffels, and grocery bags stuffed with snacks. Jordan and Pierce each held one handle of the giant cooler slung between them. They weren't identical twins, but they were similar enough that anybody meeting them knew instantly they were brothers. Both were tall, with broad shoulders, dark blond hair, and a smile that had every girl in school weak in the knees.

And at least one boy too.

The trek to the house took longer than any of them expected. At least it was a relatively cool evening for August. Still, Linsey's boyfriend Craig was whining and the sun nearly setting by the time they reached their destination.

The Gustafson house sat in the center of a small clearing, like some kind of silent queen on her throne. The powder blue paint was cracked and peeling, but she still seemed regal. Even Mother Nature seemed subservient to the house. No birds chirped. No squirrels chattered. The trees didn't rustle their leaves in the breeze as they had along the path, and the lightning bugs seemed determined to keep their distance.

Jordan and Pierce dropped the cooler and spoke at the exact same time.

"It's bigger than I expected."

"How will we get in?"

Both of them used hushed tones. Haven wondered at that. After all, nobody was close enough to hear them.

Unless the stories of the ghosts were true after all.

But the question of how they'd get in was a good one. The windows on the ground floor were boarded up, and a sign on the front door announced that anybody caught trespassing inside the premises would be prosecuted.

"I don't know about this," Craig said. "What if we get busted?"

Craig's dad was a police officer, so it was safe to assume he didn't want to be caught breaking the law. Still, based on the way he eyed the house, Haven was pretty sure that wasn't what had Craig scared. Hadn't Linsey warned him about her sister's pranks?

Haven caught Linsey's exasperated expression and tried not to laugh. Then he saw the wicked look on Elise's face, and his laughter died in his throat. Craig had just set himself up as Elise's prime target. Haven almost felt sorry for the guy, but he kept his mouth shut. If he ruined Elise's game now, everybody might decide to turn around and go home. Haven wasn't about to let that happen. The twins were leaving for Ohio State University in two short weeks, and after that, he might never see Pierce again.

It was pretty much this weekend or never.

"It'll be fine," Linsey said, taking Craig's hand. "Everybody knows ghosts aren't real."

Elise twirled her keys around her finger, her bejeweled "Class of '03" key ring sparkling in the last few rays of daylight. "You'll be singing a different tune after our séance."

At nineteen, Elise was the oldest of the group—another reason Haven knew she was up to no good. Jordan and Pierce were only a year younger than her, having graduated from high school in the spring. Haven and Craig were seventeen, and Linsey was the baby at sixteen. Even if Elise liked Jordan as much as he liked her, why would she hang out with a bunch of high schoolers, if not to get a laugh at their expense?

"Hey, Jordan," Elise said, hefting a canvas duffel bag and motioning toward the front door. "Come help me with this."

It was almost comical how quickly Jordan moved to do her bidding. Haven wondered for a moment if Elise planned to recruit Jordan as a conspirator in her little campaign to scare the rest of them. He watched them put their heads together and noted the cunning glint in Elise's eye. No. She'd leave Jordan in the dark. She wouldn't give up such a willing victim, especially knowing anything she said to him was likely to reach Pierce's ears ten seconds later.

Haven dropped his sleeping bag, slipped his backpack off, and rolled his shoulders, glad to be free of the weight. Linsey and Craig had moved a few feet away and seemed to be having a quiet but intense argument. Elise and Jordan were on the front porch of the house, completely engrossed in each other. That left Haven alone with Pierce.

Which was exactly what he'd hoped for when he agreed to this ridiculous plan.

"What do you think?" Pierce asked, coming to stand next to Haven. "Is it haunted?"

"That's what they say."

Pierce was two or three inches taller than Haven. Their arms touched, and not for the first time, Haven found himself wondering if those touches were accidental or intentional.

"I know what they say. But do you believe it?"

Haven didn't know how to answer. Haunted or not, he didn't care. Standing so close to Pierce, he had the wild, exhilarating feeling that everything in his life had been leading him to this moment with Pierce in this strangely quiet clearing. He was sure this one night would change his life.

Years later, he'd look back and marvel at that surety. He was right. That night did change his life.

But not in the way he'd hoped.

CHAPTER 2

Present Day

Haven always expected he'd see Pierce Hunter again. He was fairly certain he knew how it would happen too. The only question was when.

After the incident at the Gustafson house, and the frenzied investigation that followed, everything had fallen apart. The last time he'd seen Pierce, they'd argued bitterly over the events of that night. Then they'd gone their separate ways. The Hunter twins had left for college and Haven had returned to Hobbsburg High School for his senior year. A year later, he'd been the one leaving for college. And during the years he spent at West Virginia University, both his parents and Linsey and Elise's parents had moved away from Hobbsburg.

There were just too many memories there.

Haven had never gone back to his hometown or to the Gustafson house. He didn't know if the Hunters had ever returned, or if their parents still lived there. The only thing Haven knew for certain was that Jordan Hunter was a murderer. Someday, Jordan would be arrested. And when that happened, both Haven and Pierce would be in the courtroom for the trial, albeit on opposite sides of aisle.

So yes, Haven assumed he'd have to face Pierce again on some dreary, distant day. What he hadn't anticipated was turning on the TV one lazy afternoon and finding the twins starring in their own TV show, *Paranormal Hunters*.

As crazy as it sounded, Pierce and Jordan had become professional paranormal investigators.

"Their journey began years ago, in a house everybody knew was haunted," the voice-over intro began. "One night, one ghostly encounter, and a mystery that was never solved. Now the Hunter brothers are determined to find the truth about ghosts, haunted houses…" Here, there was a dramatic pause in the narration, a crescendo of the spooky music, and a close-up of the brothers standing back to back with their arms crossed. "…and what lies beyond this realm."

The twins were still gorgeous, and still naturally charismatic enough to draw in fans. Jordan, it seemed, was the believer. Pierce acted as the skeptic, cheerfully debunking as many of their findings as he could. Sometimes the show struck Haven as borderline ridiculous. Other times, it creeped him right the hell out. Either way, *Paranormal Hunters* was surprisingly entertaining.

An even bigger surprise came in the summer between the second and third seasons of *Paranormal Hunters*, when Pierce suddenly contacted Haven out of the blue.

It started with an email.

> *Haven,*
>
> *I know it's been a long time, but I'd really like to talk. Can I call you?*
>
> *Pierce*

Haven was midway through a round of edits on his latest novel when the email arrived. He'd rented a quaint little cabin in Downeast Maine for the summer, determined to do a bit of research for his next story in between edits, although, in truth, he hadn't done much more than read and watch the boats move in and out of the harbor. Outside, the day was warm and sunny, but after reading Pierce's email, Haven was instantly lost in his memory of a dark, chilly room in a house that had long been rumored to be haunted.

Pierce wanted to talk to him. Was it about what had happened that night? Was he finally ready to accept the truth about his twin?

Haven's fingers shook as he typed a quick reply. He didn't say much. Just gave his cell number and hit send.

It had been twelve long years. Maybe justice was finally about to be served.

"Hey, Haven," Pierce said, over the phone. "Long time no talk, huh?"

It hadn't taken long for him to call, and even though Haven had given Pierce the green light, he'd debated not answering the phone at all once it rang. But now here he was, clutching his iPhone to the side of his face, his heart racing the way it always had where Pierce was concerned. "Yeah," was all he managed to say. "Twelve years."

"How've you been?"

"Uh...okay, I guess." But as sucky at small talk as ever, it seemed.

"I'm a big fan, you know. I've read all your books. That last one, about the house with the haunted basement? I'm telling you, it scared the crap out of me."

Nearly every one of Haven's books had grown from one of Elise's wild tales. If he had it to do it all over again, he'd have published them under her name. But at the time—back when he'd finished that first manuscript and sent it in to an agent—it hadn't occurred to him. Sometimes he felt like a fraud for having stolen all his stories from her, but he tried to look at it as his way of honoring her. Every book he published was dedicated to Elise.

Still, the fact that Pierce had read his books surprised him.

And, in that moment, the pieces fell into place. Haven made his living writing horror stories with a paranormal twist.

Pierce and Jordan were professional paranormal investigators. And they'd once spent a night together in a notorious haunted house.

He knew now why Pierce was calling.

"I don't know if you've seen our show?" Pierce asked. "*Paranormal Hunters?*"

"Once or twice." Actually, he'd watched every single episode, partly just to have an excuse to stare at Pierce, partly in hopes of catching Jordan in some kind of lie.

"Well, here's the thing…some teenage girl in Hobbsburg recently reported a paranormal encounter at the old Gustafson house. Our producers got wind of it, found out it was *the* house—you know, the one we talk about in the intro—and now they're determined to do an episode there."

Haven's throat was so tight and dry he had a hard time forcing any sound past his lips. "Oh?" was all he managed.

"We start shooting in two weeks, and the thing is, well… I'd really like to have you there."

"Why?"

"Officially? Because you were there. And because having the world-famous horror author Haven Sage on our show will be great publicity for both you and us."

"World famous" was probably a bit of a stretch, but Haven let the flattery lie. "And unofficially?"

"Because after all these years, I think it's time we got some answers." He paused for a moment, but when Haven didn't respond, he went on. "The producers are contacting Linsey and Craig too. They're turning this into a two-part event, centered around finding the truth about what happened that night."

"What happened had nothing to do with ghosts."

"I know. You and I can agree on that, at least."

"And what about Jordan?" Just saying the name made his skin crawl.

Pierce seemed hesitant to answer, and Haven knew why. Pierce knew that Haven blamed Jordan for Elise's disappearance. "He's a believer," he confessed at last. "He has been ever since that night. He thinks Joseph got to Elise."

"That's ridiculous."

"I know."

"Then why—"

Pierce sighed. "Look, Haven..." Haven was surprised at how sad and uncertain he sounded. "I don't want to argue. Not about this. Especially not over the phone."

Haven almost laughed. "What? You want to save the arguments for in person? Or maybe for the cameras?"

"That's not quite what I meant, but yeah. We all have our theories. Jordan blames a ghost. You blame him. I blame Craig. But the truth is, the case went cold ages ago."

"That special on the ID Network generated a lot of calls to the hotline."

"But did any of them pan out?"

Haven didn't want to answer that. The tiny bit of hope the show had generated had resulted in more than a dozen dead ends. "They say they're working new leads every day."

"Do you truly believe that?"

It hurt to say it, but he decided to be honest. "No. That's just what they're supposed to say."

They fell silent. Outside, the gulls swooped over the bay, calling to one another. Across the road from Haven's cabin, a group of teens lounged on the dock in swimsuits and cutoff shorts. Sunlight flashed off sunglass lenses and highlighted smooth, tan arms and thighs as they laughed and flirted, oblivious to how quickly their world could change. Haven closed his eyes, not wanting to see them. Not wanting to remember how young and carefree and clueless he and his friends had once been.

Wherever Pierce was, Haven imagined him running his hand through his hair, trying to find the right words to say.

"You want justice for Elise, don't you?" Pierce finally asked.

"More than anything."

"Then meet me in Hobbsburg. Help me finally find the truth. Between us, we'll figure out what happened to Elise, one way or another."

"And if the truth is that I was right all along?"

Pierce hesitated, but only for a moment. "Like I said, one way or another. So what do you say? You in, or are you out?"

Haven didn't hesitate. "I'm in."

Pierce had said the producers of *Paranormal Hunters* would contact Linsey, so rather than call himself and spill the beans, Haven once again waited for his phone to ring.

The call came late the following afternoon, while Haven was on the wrap-around patio of his stupidly picturesque Maine rental, sipping an iced latte. The teens from the day before were gone, and the dock seemed empty and desolate without them.

"Can you believe it?" Linsey said immediately. "Can you believe those assholes are going to make money off Elise's disappearance?"

Haven hadn't quite thought of it in those terms, and the implication made him squirm. No matter what he thought of Jordan, it seemed the years hadn't lessened his innate instinct to defend Pierce.

"Will you go?" he asked.

She sighed heavily, and he pictured her standing in her kitchen in Frederick, Maryland, her brown hair pulled back in a ponytail and her fist perched on her hip. "Two weeks from now is my due date." Haven had halfway forgotten the baby about to be born. He quickly amended his mental image of his cousin by adding an enormously swollen belly. "Even if I wanted to go, which I don't, Josh would throw a fit."

Josh was her husband, and given the difficulties she'd had delivering their first child three years earlier, Haven thought Josh had a right to worry.

"What about you?" Linsey asked. "Will you go?"

"I said I would."

"Good. I'm glad somebody reasonable will be there."

He hadn't expected her approval, but he was glad to have it. "I'll do my best." He debated his next question for a moment before blurting it out. "What about Craig? Do you think he'll be there?"

"He still lives in Hobbsburg, so I don't see why not."

"He does?" Haven tried to keep his tone casual. He knew Linsey's break-up with Craig had been hard on her. "You keep in touch?"

"Only on Facebook. But I know he's a cop there now, working for his dad." She went quiet, and Haven knew she was thinking about Elise. "I still wonder, you know? I still wonder if he had anything to do with it."

"I don't think he did. I think—"

"I know you blame Jordan, and I get it, but Craig's behavior that night..."

Haven waited. When it became clear she'd run out of gas, he prodded her. "What about it?"

He heard the distinct sound of a chair leg scraping across a wooden floor, then another sigh as Linsey lowered her unwieldy bulk into it. "The thing is... I actually wonder if Elise wasn't having some kind of fling with him. Sometimes I wonder if he went to hook up with her that night."

Haven sat back in his Adirondack chair, stunned. "Are you crazy?"

"Probably." He heard a bit of laughter in her voice. "It probably wasn't Craig, but the thing is, I've always thought there was another man."

"For Elise, you mean? You think she was dating somebody at the time? Why didn't you say anything?"

"Because I didn't really know. She never came right out and said it. It was just more the way she was acting. Like, getting all dolled up when she was supposedly just meeting Judy Roberts for a movie. Sneaking out after Mom and Dad had gone to bed. Things like that. Whoever she was seeing, I think it'd been going on for several weeks, but she never said anything out loud."

"And none of her friends knew about it, either," Haven said, remembering. Elise's friends had all been questioned multiple times, but a secret boyfriend had never come up.

"Exactly. And you know, it wasn't like a Nancy Drew novel. Elise didn't leave behind a journal full of secrets or anything. At the time, I figured if she was actually seeing somebody, they'd come forward. I mean, you know how high schoolers are when somebody dies. They start telling everybody how well they knew that person, making every date sound like a wedding engagement. So I figured it'd come out on its own. And then the whole thing happened with Lance Gustafson, and there was just so much going on…"

"So you didn't think it was important?"

"It's more like, I convinced myself I was wrong, and that she hadn't been dating anybody. I kept thinking, why would she have kept it a secret, not only from me, but from Mom and Dad, and from her friends as well? And why didn't the boyfriend ever come forward? Because I'd made him up, that's why. But then a year or two ago, Craig sent me a friend request on Facebook, and I started thinking, what if it was him? What if that was the reason she kept it from me?"

Haven thought back to that night, trying to pinpoint something that might support Linsey's accusation, but he came up empty. Elise had seemed completely engrossed in Jordan Hunter.

Had it all been an act to hide the fact that she was sleeping with her sister's boyfriend?

No. Haven couldn't imagine Elise doing anything that cruel. But he trusted Linsey's instincts. It was entirely possible Elise *had* been seeing somebody. But if so, who? And why hadn't he ever come forward?

The answer seemed obvious.

Whoever he was, he was also Elise's murderer.

CHAPTER 3

Twelve Years Ago

Somehow, Elise got the front door open. Haven wouldn't think to wonder about that until much later. At the moment, he was just happy to get inside and put down his things.

They stepped into an entryway with stairs up one side. A tacky wrought-iron chandelier with no bulbs dominated the overhead space. The living room sat to their left, large and gloomy. A few rays of waning sunlight slashed between the boards over the window, but it wasn't enough to dispel the shadows. The house was empty, but surprisingly clean inside. Technically, it'd been for sale for more than twenty years, although Haven doubted anybody had inquired on it in ages.

Still, it didn't *feel* haunted.

"I'm starving," Craig said.

The rest heartily agreed. The hike from the car had stoked their appetites. They sat cross-legged on the floor, munching on chips, sandwiches, and cold fried chicken. Elise had brought along a couple of six-packs of beer, which she, Jordan, and Pierce happily broke into. Haven opted for a Dr Pepper, wanting to keep his wits about him as much as possible. Linsey did the same. Craig split the difference by opening one of each. By the time they finished eating, the room was almost totally dark. They dug through their bags looking for flashlights, laughing about how they should have done it before the light failed them. Haven wished he'd thought to bring one of his dad's kerosene lanterns.

"It's spooky, isn't it?" Elise asked, shining her flashlight around the room.

"We could light a fire," Linsey said, pointing her flashlight beam at the fireplace.

Haven thought it was a good idea, but Jordan shook his head. "There's no telling when they last swept that chimney. We'd be in big trouble if we burned the house down."

"And started a forest fire to boot," Pierce added.

The whole group seemed to slump, with the possibility of a roaring fire taken from them.

"Let's explore a bit," Elise suggested. "That way we'll know where we want to sleep later."

The ground floor held a kitchen, dining room, a small office, and a claustrophobic den that might have been dubbed "cozy" on a better day. There was also a bathroom, but a test of the faucet told them the water to the house had been turned off, and they all reluctantly agreed that any "business" would have to be done outside in the woods.

They dragged their bags up the stairs, past the sad chandelier. The second floor held another bathroom and four large bedrooms. The windows here hadn't been boarded up. It was nearly full dark outside, but being able to see the woods and the sky meant the bedrooms felt less oppressive than the rooms on the ground floor.

Linsey and Craig took the master bedroom. Jordan and Elise took the one next to it.

"Guess that leaves us as roommates," Pierce said to Haven. "Which room should we take?"

"Doesn't matter to me." He was just glad Pierce was open to the idea of them sharing. The thought of sleeping alone in one of the empty rooms gave him the creeps.

They tossed their gear into the smaller of the two remaining bedrooms, then followed the rest of the group back down the stairs to the living room, where Elise was already setting out candles in a circle on the living room floor.

Haven exchanged a glance with Linsey and knew they were both hoping to squash this stupid séance idea. Elise would do her best to scare them all anyway, but it seemed unwise to give her too much rein.

Linsey spoke first. "Give it up, Elise. You don't even know how to hold a séance."

"Sure I do. I looked it up online."

"I once read how to fly an airplane online," Haven said. "That doesn't make me a pilot."

"Don't be such a chicken, Haven," Elise said. "I swear, you've been a 'fraidy-cat ever since you were a kid."

Haven's cheeks burned. He was hyper aware of Pierce standing next to him, listening to his cousin tease him. Trying to argue with Elise would only make him look more childish. He glanced Linsey's direction. The look she gave him was sympathetic, but she seemed resigned to letting Elise have her way.

As usual, there seemed to be little point in resisting.

Elise had gathered a hodgepodge of candles—a few votives in glass cups; some in jars, with labels declaring long-lasting fruity scents; and a couple of long tapers in silver holders that had obviously been taken from her mom's china cabinet. They all watched in silence as Elise lit them. Finally, she sat back on her heels and looked up at them.

"What are you waiting for? Everybody sit inside the circle, close enough that you can hold hands. We should be boy-girl, boy-girl, but we're short on girls."

"Pierce counts as a girl," Jordan said.

Pierce laughed, clearly unfazed by his brother's teasing.

Once they were situated—and Haven was pleased at how easy it had been to make sure he sat beside Pierce—Elise placed three matching votives in the center and lit them. Next, she produced a green glass bottle, about the size of a bottle of wine, but shaped differently. She poured a bit of liquid from the bottle into the cap and placed it in the center of the circle, beside the candles.

"This is our offering to the spirits." She handed the bottle to Craig, who sat on her right. "Take a drink and pass it on."

Craig did as he was told, grimacing as he did. "That's nasty. It tastes like black licorice."

"Is it Jäger?" Jordan asked.

"No." Linsey tilted the bottle so she could read the label in the candlelight. "It's absinthe." She turned to Elise. "Mom and Dad brought this back from France. You'll be in so much trouble if they find out you took it."

Elise waved her off. "It's been in that cabinet for, what? Ten years now? They drank a bit that first night home and haven't touched it since then. They've forgotten all about it."

Linsey didn't look convinced, but she took a drink and passed the bottle to Haven. Haven would have bet his last dollar she'd barely wet her lips with it. He did the same, then passed it on.

"So," Elise said, rubbing her hands together and glancing around the circle. "Let's talk first about what happened in this house."

"Everybody knows—" Linsey started to say, but Elise cut her off.

"Jordan and Pierce have only lived here a couple of years now." She turned to Jordan. "Do you know the whole story?"

"I heard somebody was killed here."

"Right here," Elise said, leaning into their circle, "in this very room."

The announcement had the intended result. They all glanced around, as if expecting to find a body hiding in the corner.

"The legend starts way before that, though," Elise said, warming to her story. "Back when the Gustafsons first built this house in the 1800s. They were told not to build here, because it was an Indian burial ground, but they did it anyway."

Haven frowned, trying to remember if he'd ever heard anything about an Indian burial ground in the area. He had a feeling Elise was making that part up.

"They say the house was haunted from the very beginning," Elise went on. "Then, twenty-four years ago, the owners died." She pointed at the ceiling. "Old Lady Gustafson and her husband both died in their bed, right upstairs. Some say they died of fright, though no one knows why."

Haven exchanged another glance with Linsey. This was another part of the story he'd never heard before, and, again, he wondered if any of it was true.

"After they died, the house passed to Frank and Isabel Gustafson. At first, Isabel wanted to live out here. But after spending a few nights in the house, she said it gave her the creeps, so they decided to put it on the market. Their real estate agent hired one of those people to come in and make the place look just right—"

"A stager," Pierce said.

"Right. So they took out all the personal items, but there was still furniture in all the rooms. But then, one Sunday..." The bottle was on its third round now, and Elise scooted marginally closer to the center of the circle. The rest of them instinctively followed suit. "It was the day after prom, and the prom queen, Cassie Kennedy, didn't come home.

"Her date said they'd split up at the after-prom party. He wasn't sure where she'd gone. Everybody just assumed she was at one of her friends' houses, sleeping it off. When she still wasn't home by dinner, her parents flipped out. The whole town went out looking for her, but nobody knew where she was. Then, that next Monday, some people from out of town came here to view the house, and they found her. Right. Here."

She pointed to the center of the circle. Haven shivered, despite himself. He had to give Elise credit. She was good at this kind of thing.

"How'd she die?" Pierce asked.

"She was slaughtered. There was blood everywhere. That's why they pulled up the carpet and left only bare boards. But look." She pointed to a small smudge of darkness at her knee. "In some places, the blood soaked all the way through to the wood."

"Who killed her?" Jordan asked. "The prom king?"

It seemed to be asked halfway in jest, but Elise answered earnestly. "The police looked into him, but everybody had seen him at the party on prom night, right up until two in the morning, and then his parents said he'd come straight home. So the next thing they did was find out who had keys to the house. There were only two sets. One belonged to the real estate agent, who was this gray-haired, little old lady. And the other belonged to the people who owned the house, Frank and Isabel Gustafson."

"So, it was Frank?" Pierce asked.

"No. When the police went to their house, they found out he was out of town on business. He had a rock-solid alibi, all the way in New York. And Isabel couldn't find the keys. They weren't in the drawer, where they were supposed to be. That only left three people."

"Their sons," Craig said.

Elise nodded. "Right. One son, in particular. See, the oldest, Robert, was away at college. The youngest, Lance—"

"Wait," Pierce said. "You mean Mr. Gustafson? The English teacher at the high school?"

Elise smiled. "That's him. He's the baby of the family. He was only nine at the time, so that pretty much put him in the clear. But the middle brother, Joseph, was seventeen."

"My dad knew him," Craig said quietly. "Joseph was a couple of years behind him in school, but he says everybody knew he was a trouble-maker."

"He was," Elise said. "He'd already been busted for vandalism, for breaking and entering, and for underage consumption of alcohol. He had no alibi for that night. Everybody expected the police to arrest him for Cassie's murder, but they never had the chance." She waited, glancing around the circle. They all leaned a bit closer. "Joseph hung himself." She pointed over Haven's shoulder, to the stairs. "Right there. From the banister."

"But they know he did it?" Pierce asked.

"He left a note," Elise said, her voice hushed. "He confessed to killing Cassie. And now, they're both doomed to haunt this house together. Forever."

CHAPTER 4

Present Day

Technically, Haven lived in Pittsburgh, but only because that was where his parents lived. He hated the city and spent as little time there as possible. Ten days after talking to Pierce, he landed at Pittsburgh International Airport. He checked in with his parents, ate dinner with them both nights he was in town, but didn't tell them his purpose in Pennsylvania.

For some reason he couldn't quite explain, he didn't want them to know his plans.

He hit the Turnpike two days later, breathing a sigh of relief as he left the city behind. Once he hit Portage, he veered southeast. From there, it was only another fifteen minutes before he was back in the town of his youth.

Back home, for better or worse.

The butterflies in his stomach grew more pronounced with every mile. It was the first time he'd been back since leaving for college eleven years earlier.

Hobbsburg didn't look much different. Still the same pair of tiny motels by the highway, the same brick library on Main Street, the same swimming pool full of laughing, screaming kids. The only thing different was the giant Wal-Mart, sitting like a blue and yellow scab on the edge of town.

The *Paranormal Hunters* team had offered to put him up at the Marriott in Altoona, but Haven had opted instead to stay in Hobbsburg, For reasons he couldn't quite explain, he didn't want to be at the same motel as Pierce and Jordan. That meant Haven ended up at what had once been a Howard Johnson's Inn. When he was a kid, it had been operated by a friend of his mother. He remembered being amazed by the circular fireplace that warmed the center of the lobby. He remembered playing in the hallways while his mom and her friend drank coffee and chatted about whatever grown-ups talked about back then.

The orange roof that had once been the trademark of Howard Johnson's still remained, but the motel had a new name and a new manager. The interior had been remodeled—the fireplace had been removed, and the bright red shag carpet had been replaced with utilitarian tile. Haven felt a moment of sadness at having one more bit of his childhood erased, but there was no turning back time. The past always yielded to the present.

He had just enough time to check in and freshen up before heading for the old Gustafson house to meet up with Pierce and Jordan. His sweaty palms gripped the steering wheel as he turned off the highway onto the county road. He double-checked his hair in the rearview mirror before mentally scolding himself for being an idiot. It had been twelve years, yet he was still acting like a nervous teenager.

He slowed, looking for the rutted dirt lane that would take him to the Gustafson house. A wooden gate had been installed across the road, with a NO TRESPASSING sign nailed to it. Pierce had warned him to expect that, had told him to come through anyway, since the show had permission to film on-site. Beyond the gate, the trail was so overgrown with grass it was barely distinguishable. Only the passage of several cars before him made it possible for Haven to follow it.

The chain that had once stopped their progress was gone, although the two poles that had held it in place still stood, sad sentinels of the past. Half a mile later, Haven came to the fence that had been erected as a result of their night of trespassing. It was chain link, seven feet tall, crowned with loops of razor wire. More signs warned that trespassers would be prosecuted, although the graffiti spray-painted over them gave testament to the site's continuing allure for local teenagers. Haven wondered how the most recent group had gained access. Had they climbed the fence, or cut their way through? Haven suspected the latter.

Luckily, he didn't have to resort to anything so complicated. The gate stood open. A *Paranormal Hunters* truck and two small sedans sat in a silent row in what counted as the house's driveway. Haven parked behind them, then climbed out of his car to get his first good look at the house in twelve years.

Nothing much had changed. Maybe the paint had peeled a bit more. Maybe the front porch sagged more than it used to, but for the most part, it seemed exactly as it had that distant day, the meadow around it strangely hushed and silent. He remembered standing in almost this same spot, with Pierce at his side. He remembered the secret hopes he'd fostered that night, his surety that his life would never be the same. He recalled with aching clarity the nervousness, the delicious apprehension that had twisted his stomach into knots.

He might have stood there forever, lost in the memory of it, if the front door hadn't opened right at that moment.

Pierce stepped out into the sunlight, waving. Haven had seen him a hundred times on his television screen, it hadn't prepared him for this moment, seeing Pierce again in real life, wearing jeans and a faded *Paranormal Hunters* T-shirt, his blond hair neatly trimmed, yet somehow still messy. He seemed so rugged and solid and *real*, in a way nothing else in the clearing did.

"You made it," Pierce said.

"I did."

"Well, don't just stand there. Come on in."

Haven forced his feet to move. The sun flashed off his glasses, making him blink. The tall grass brushed his legs as he crossed the open space, feeling Pierce's gaze on him the whole way. Pierce had always had a way of watching him that filled Haven with a mixed sense of elation and self-conscious nervousness. Forget butterflies in his stomach. This felt more like a confused swarm of bees. He climbed the rickety steps, and finally found himself face-to-face with the past.

Pierce hadn't shaved in a day or two. The bit of growth looked good on him, accentuating his blue eyes and the rough planes of his face. Haven had apparently grown a bit since that summer, because their height difference wasn't as pronounced as it had once been. But the way Haven's world seemed to shift on its axis at the sight of him? That hadn't changed at all.

"It's good to see you," Pierce said. Haven had wondered whether Pierce would hug him or shake his hand, but Pierce did neither. He opted instead for smacking Haven lightly on the shoulder. "You look good."

"Thanks. So do you." Apparently, his penchant for spouting inane bullshit hadn't changed either.

"Come inside. We have a lot to discuss."

The living room looked much as it had before, except dustier. Boards still covered the windows, blocking out the sunlight. An amoebic, oily stain on the bare floor showed where a candle from their séance had spilled. Haven glanced uneasily toward the stairway, as if expecting to see Joseph hanging there, but he found only cobwebs clinging to the dingy chandelier.

But the house had been silent back then. Now, cheerful voices emanated from one of the ground level rooms down the hallway. Heavy footsteps on the hardwood floor told Haven whoever owned those voices was headed his way.

Jordan was the first to arrive, and Haven scowled, trying to tamp down the anger he felt whenever he thought of Pierce's twin.

"Hey, Haven," Jordan said, sounding almost apologetic. Like his brother, he opted not to shake Haven's hand. Unlike his brother, he seemed a bit ill at ease. "Glad you could make it."

Two men and a woman followed behind him. They ran quickly through introductions. Jeremy, the director, in his forties and carrying a belly that hid his belt. Todd, the cameraman, in his early twenties, on the geeky side of cute. And Justine, the technical assistant, with tattoos covering her arms, and her long red hair looped into a do reminiscent of a 1960's pinup girl.

Jeremy and Todd were on their way to town for hamburgers and batteries—a combination that had Haven scratching his head—and left with little more than a wave. Justine took drink orders from Jordan, who apparently remembered Haven's penchant for Dr Pepper, before heading out to the production trailer.

"We were sorry Linsey couldn't come," Jordan said, once he, Pierce, and Haven were alone again. "She would have been a great addition to the show."

Not because they wondered how she was doing, but because it would have been good entertainment. It annoyed Haven, but he let it go. "What about Craig?" he asked.

Pierce shook his head. "I think he would have done it, but he's a cop here now, and his boss said no."

"Isn't his boss also his dad?"

"He is," Jordan said, his tone making it clear he didn't hold the elder Fuller in much regard. "Chief Daavettila had a stroke about eight years ago, and never fully recovered. Craig's dad took over as chief of police in Hobbsburg. He wasn't all that keen on us being here at all, to tell you the truth. He tried to keep it from happening. Luckily for us, it wasn't up to him. But we're under strict orders to keep things as low-key as possible. They don't want folks learning we're out here and turning it into a party." He touched the side of his head nervously, as if checking to make sure his hair hadn't moved. It hadn't. As always, it was perfectly moussed into place. He apparently found it acceptable, because he gave Haven a hesitant smile and gestured to the back of the house.

"Why don't you come on back? We can at least sit while we talk."

The *Paranormal Hunters* crew had set up a sort of home base in the ground-floor office of the house. The window was still boarded up, but the wooden floor had been swept clean, and the cobwebs cleared from the corners. A couple of rickety card tables and half a dozen folding chairs occupied the center of the room. It was at one of these that Haven settled with Pierce directly across from him and Jordan on one of the sides in between. Pierce sat close to the table, looking confident and comfortable with his elbows resting on it as he leaned toward Haven. Jordan, on the other hand, kept his chair a few inches back, his arms crossed over his chest.

Understandable, Haven supposed, since he knew Haven thought he was a murderer.

"The first thing we'll do when filming starts," Pierce said, "is go over the history of this house."

He paused, as Justine arrived with three cans of pop and a thick manila folder.

"Do you need anything else?" she asked, as she placed the items in the center of the table. The question was aimed directly at Jordan, as if Pierce and Haven weren't even there.

"Not right now," Jordan said, winking at her. "Thank you."

Justine seemed delighted by the bit of attention. Haven clenched his teeth, wanting to jump up and warn her that Jordan was dangerous, and the best thing she could do was stay far, far away from him. But she was gone again before he mustered his nerve.

"The thing you have to realize," Pierce said, as he cracked open his can of Dr Pepper, "is that every house has two stories. There's the one that's real, and then there's the one that all the locals *think* is real."

"What do you mean?" Haven asked.

It was Jordan who answered. "Urban legends, essentially. They're more powerful than the truth. More accurate too, sometimes."

"An urban legend is more accurate than facts?" Haven asked, incredulous.

"Well," Pierce said, "take this house, for example. Remember the story Elise told us about its history?"

"I do." He remembered the doubts he'd had, even then. It was time to finally clear the air about exactly the type of person Elise had been. "Look," he said, leaning forward to match Pierce's posture. "I'm not sure if you guys ever realized what a prankster Elise was. She was completely full of it. I mean, she was tons of fun, and I loved her, but—"

The twins burst out laughing, cutting him off. They exchanged a glance Haven couldn't interpret.

"What's so funny?"

The brothers glanced at each other again. They'd always done this, seemingly sharing some kind of silent dialog that had once made Haven wonder if they could read each other's minds.

It was Jordan who answered, with an awkward shrug. "Just that Pierce was pretty worried about how to break that news to you—that Elise was full of shit."

"You knew?" Haven asked Pierce.

Pierce shook his head. "Not back then, no. But a couple of years later, when Jordan and I started getting serious about the paranormal investigation, I did some research." He set his can of pop aside and began flipping through the papers and photos in the manila folder. "First, there was no Indian burial ground. That was complete nonsense. I mean, yeah, maybe a Native American once died in the area. The same could be said of every inch of land in the United States. But there's absolutely no record of this chunk of land ever being special, in any way whatsoever. The house wasn't even built in the 1800s. It was built in 1939." He selected a photo and slid it across the table to Haven. It showed the house they were sitting in, only with a fresh coat of paint and a front porch that didn't sag. A young couple stood in front of it, arms around each other's waists, their smiles bright and fearless.

"These are the Gustafsons?"

"Yep. But they didn't die in the house like Elise said." He handed Haven another photo of what Haven assumed was the same couple, only taken at least three decades later. This one looked like something from the portrait department of JC Penney, with a backdrop of poorly painted aspen trees. "The husband died of a heart attack in 1977 while buying lottery tickets at Mini-Mart. His wife died three years later of heart failure, but by that point, she'd been living in a nursing home for the better part of two years. They never reported anything unusual about the house."

"Wow," Haven said, shaking his head. "I can't say any of that surprises me."

"One more thing. Remember how Elise said Cassie had been slaughtered? That there was blood everywhere?"

Haven nodded, remembering the stain on the floor next to Elise's knee.

"Well, that part isn't true either."

"So what actually happened?"

"She was strangled," Pierce replied. "With the tie from her prom dress."

"The tie?" As stupid as it was, Haven was picturing a man's necktie, but that couldn't be right.

Pierce flipped through a few more pages before finding the one he wanted. Not a photo this time, but a color copy of one, depicting a smiling young couple. The girl wore a floor-length yellow dress. The boy wore a tux. Pierce pointed to the girl's waist. "See the ribbon there? It tied in the back of the dress."

"That's what he strangled her with?"

Pierce nodded. "She'd been sexually assaulted. The dress was ripped in several places. But despite what Elise said, there was no blood."

Haven couldn't take his eyes off Cassie's face. She looked so young and innocent. The photo had been taken in front of a floor-to-ceiling teal curtains, the arm of a sofa just visible in the corner of the frame. "This was taken by her parents?" he asked.

"His, actually," Jordan said, his voice quiet. "After her date picked her up, he took her back to his house, because his mom didn't trust Cassie's mom to ever give her copies of the ones she'd taken."

Such an odd little detail to be discussing all these years later. How petty the question of pictures must have seemed by the end of the weekend, when Cassie still wasn't home. She looked so happy. So naive. Nobody could have known that only a few hours later, she'd be dead.

Nobody except Joseph Gustafson, at least.

CHAPTER 5

Twelve Years Ago

Elise's dramatic announcement that Joseph Gustafson and Cassie Kennedy still haunted the house received mixed reviews. Jordan laughed. Craig shifted nervously. Pierce betrayed no emotions whatsoever.

Haven exchanged a glance with Linsey. Her expression mirrored his exact thoughts. She seemed to be saying, "Well, here we go. Let the games begin."

Craig was the only one still drinking the absinthe. The bottle was now only half full. Haven had barely sipped it, the times it'd come to him. He hadn't seen Elise drink from it at all. She just passed it to the next person each time, without interrupting her story.

"So the house has just been sitting here ever since?" Jordan asked.

Elise nodded. "Nobody wants to buy it. A few people have looked, but they've all felt a strange presence." She glanced around the room. "Don't you guys feel it? Like, a kind of dark energy in the room." She didn't wait for them to confirm or deny this wild claim. "Some say they've seen a girl in a ripped prom dress, standing right there at the window. That's why they boarded it up. And some say that if you listen"—she lowered her voice even more—"you can hear the *creak, creak, creak* of the rope on the banister, as Joseph swings back and forth, back and forth."

A shiver crept up Haven's spine despite his determination not to let Elise's story get to him. He resisted the urge to look over his shoulder at the stairs, although he noticed everybody else glance that way.

"We may see him," Elise went on. "Tonight. When we call for his and Cassie's spirits. We might see his body, hanging in the air."

Haven swallowed, trying to remind himself that Elise was full of crap. He couldn't seem to keep his eyes off the small spot on the floorboards, which she claimed was Cassie Kennedy's blood. He glanced around the circle. They'd all scooted closer to the center as Elise told her story, their knees almost touching now. The bottle of absinthe sat behind Craig, not quite empty and seemingly forgotten. Outside their circle of candles, the room was lost to shadow.

"Okay," Elise said. "Let's all join hands."

Haven wiped his palms on his jeans first, not wanting Pierce to be too grossed out. Linsey was on Haven's left. Her fingers felt like ice. Pierce's, on his right, were comfortably warm.

"It's important that we not break the circle," Elise told them. "Okay. Now, we have to chant together. 'Spirits of the past, come to the light. Move among us on this night.' Ready?"

Everybody squirmed, all of them feeling too self-conscious already to start chanting together. Linsey laughed nervously. "This is stupid, Elise."

"Yeah, what's next?" Craig asked. "Singing 'Kumbaya'? Maybe a game of Light as a Feather, Stiff as a Board?"

"I thought only girls played that game," Linsey said.

"Guys!" Elise said. "This is serious. Everybody knows Joseph and Cassie died here. Everybody knows their spirits are trapped in this house. We can't joke about their deaths."

Haven bit his cheek to keep from laughing. "Maybe you can chant alone?" he suggested.

"It won't work. You guys have to say it too." She scowled around the circle at them. "This is why we came here, remember? You all wanted to have a séance. Are you going to chicken out now?"

"You're the one who wanted the séance," Linsey said under her breath. "Not us."

"Well, are you going to play along or not?"

Haven was about to say "or not," but Jordan spoke first. "Okay, okay. Settle down. We'll chant along. What do we say again?"

"'Spirits of the past, come to the light. Move among us on this night.'"

Jordan took a deep breath, then said it with her. "Spirits of the past, come to the light. Move among us on this night."

Pierce was next, and then, as if they were passing it like the bottle of absinthe around the circle, they joined in, one by one.

"Spirits of the past, come to the light. Move among us on this night. Spirits of the past, come to the light. Move among us on this night."

They chanted it a few more times, falling into a hushed synchronicity, all of them watching the candles in the middle of the circle, until...

"Spirits of the past, come to the light—"

The flames flickered.

They all seemed to draw breath as one, their chant forgotten.

"They're here," Elise whispered.

Pierce's hand tightened on Haven's. Or maybe he was the one who'd suddenly gripped harder. His heart tripped along in his chest, somehow too fast and too quiet at the same time.

"Joseph?" Elise called, raising her voice. "Cassie? Are you with us?"

They waited, quiet and tense.

A sudden creak from the direction of the stairs made them all gasp and turn toward the sound. Haven half expected to see a body swinging from the banister, but he could barely make out the line of the staircase. The house creaked again, as if coming to life around them. Old houses always creaked and groaned. Had it been making those noises all along, but he was only now noticing it? Or was there really something else going on?

"Who's here?" Elise asked. "Knock once for Cassie, twice for Joseph."

They waited another breathless second, and then—

Knock.

They all jumped, then chuckled self-consciously.

"That was just the house creaking," Linsey said. "Or a branch hitting the roof."

"How else do you expect them to communicate, Linsey?" Elise asked. "I mean, there's nothing in here for them to use."

"You're the one who Googled 'séances' and became an expert overnight. You tell me."

The house creaked again. This time, the sound seemed to come from the other side of the circle, behind Craig. Everybody jumped, like they had before, but this time, nobody laughed.

"Oh my God." Elise was practically whispering. "Did you hear that?"

"Hear what?" Linsey asked.

"I thought I heard footsteps coming down the stairs."

"You did not," Haven countered.

"I did. Listen."

They all froze, waiting. The seconds ticked by. The house constantly popped and moaned. Outside, trees rustled. Haven wasn't sure he'd even be able to hear footsteps over the pounding of his heart.

"There!" Elise whispered.

"I heard it!" Craig whispered back.

"You two are full of shit." But Linsey didn't sound so sure of herself.

"Did anybody else hear it?" Haven asked. He hated the way his voice shook.

"I'm not sure." Pierce sounded as unnerved as Haven felt.

"Are you here?" Elise asked, her voice tremulous. But unlike Pierce, Haven thought Elise's nervous apprehension was all an act. "Cassie? Joseph?"

Haven had to remind himself to breathe. On his left, Linsey's fingers were still cold against his. On the other side, Pierce was gripping his hand so hard, it was beginning to ache.

"We need to give them a way to communicate," Elise said. "We'll have to let them speak through me. The article I read said this can be dangerous—"

"It sounds like a bad idea," Craig said, but Elise ignored him.

"It's obviously the only way." She turned to Jordan. "You'll have to ask the questions, once Cassie's taken control of my body." She sat up a bit straighter and called out, as if to somebody down the hallway, "Use me to communicate. Take possession of me, Cassie."

"I don't like this," Linsey whispered, but Haven wasn't sure anybody else heard her.

"Let's start chanting again," Elise said. "Spirits of the past, come to the light. Move among us on this night. Spirits of the past, come to the light..."

They all took up the chant again. They hadn't exactly been enthusiastic the first time around, but they were considerably less so now.

"...Move among us on this night. Spirits of the past, come to the light..."

Haven's backside was beginning to hurt from sitting so long on the hard, wooden floor. Pierce was still gripping his hand way too tight. Haven shifted his weight around, trying to get comfortable again. He flexed the fingers of his right hand, and Pierce jumped, as if he'd forgotten they were holding hands. Pierce loosened his grip without breaking the chant, but he glanced sideways at Haven, giving him an apologetic smile that made Haven's stomach do wonderfully uncomfortable things.

"Spirits of the past, come to the light. Move among us on this night. Spirits of the past, come to the light…"

Haven wondered exactly how long they'd have to keep this up.

That was when Elise threw her head back and let out a blood-curdling scream.

CHAPTER 6

Present Day

"So most of what Elise told us that night was fiction." It was more a statement than a question. It didn't surprise him that Elise had exaggerated the facts in order to scare them all. But rather than confirm Haven's words, Pierce glanced toward his brother.

Jordan cleared his throat and sat forward. "Well, this is what I mean when I say that sometimes urban legends are more accurate than facts."

It still made no sense to Haven. He looked to Pierce for clarification.

"What he means is that paranormal encounters are rarely recorded as history," Pierce said. "It gets brushed off as rumors or fabrications. But the fact remains that in the years between Cassie's murder and the night we spent in this house, there were several reports of ...*activity*."

Haven couldn't believe what he was hearing. "'Activity'? You mean ghosts?"

"Exactly." Jordan stared at Haven, as if daring him to argue.

Pierce's answer was more hesitant. "Multiple people over the years have reported seeing the specter of a girl in a long dress standing in the window of the house."

"So Elise was right about that part? That's why they boarded them up?"

Pierce and Jordan exchanged a glance, then gave identical shrugs. "Maybe," Jordan said.

"Or maybe it was because people kept using the windows to break in," Pierce added. "But either way, the rumors never went away."

"What about Joseph?"

Jordan took the folder from Pierce and dug out another photo—a school photo, with the standard mottled blue background. The young man had black hair, wary eyes, and not even a hint of a smile. "One real estate agent swore she saw him hanging from the balcony, just like Elise said. Her partner insisted she'd only seen the shadow of the chandelier, but the woman who'd seen Joseph wasn't convinced. She refused to ever enter the house again. The assistant had to take over the listing."

"But that agent never saw anything unusual at all," Pierce said.

His brother shrugged as if it didn't matter. "Some people are more open to the energy than others." He gathered the photos from in front of Haven and put them back in the folder.

"The thing is," Pierce said, "none of us saw anything that night, despite the measures Elise went to in her attempt to convince us."

"What measures?"

"The absinthe," Jordan answered.

Haven smacked a hand to his forehead. "Of course! I figured she was just trying to get us drunk, but I didn't know back then that it could make you hallucinate."

Again, the bothers looked at each other, both of them smiling.

"That's the thing," Pierce said. "Everybody thinks that, but the truth is, absinthe is just alcohol."

"Really?" Haven's knowledge of the drink mostly boiled down to having seen the movie *Moulin Rouge*. "It doesn't make you see things?"

Pierce shook his head. "Absinthe is made with wormwood, which contains thujone, and popular belief is that thujone causes hallucinations."

"But it doesn't?"

"Thujone is in all kinds of things, like sage and oregano. Have you ever hallucinated after eating a plate of your mom's spaghetti?"

"Not that I remember."

"Exactly. And the levels of thujone found in absinthe are similar. The truth is, it doesn't do a damned thing."

Jordan sat forward to join the conversation again. "Some people claim that if you have just the right brand from just the right place, or if you have the old European absinthe, what they call 'real absinthe'"—he made quotation marks with his fingers—"instead of the watered-down American varieties, you'll still trip your balls off. But it's mostly bullshit. There's just no science to back that up."

Funny how Jordan, who hunted ghosts for a living, would want scientific evidence of the effects of thujone. "So absinthe doesn't make you see things?

"No," Pierce said. "In high enough doses, thujone *can* cause seizures. But not the amount in absinthe. Even the ones that are considered to have high levels of thujone won't make you trip."

"All it does," Jordan concluded, "is what any other alcohol does—it gets you drunk."

"Then why does everybody think it's a hallucinogen?"

"Good question," Pierce said. "It's pretty high proof and it goes down easy. People tended to drink a hell of a lot of it back in the day. A lot of them were smoking opium at the same time too, so…" Pierce shrugged, smiling.

Haven sat back in his chair to think about it. "So Elise probably thought—or at least, *hoped*—the bottle of absinthe would make us hallucinate. But it didn't."

"Exactly," Pierce and Jordan said together.

"Beyond that," Pierce continued, "she was just counting on what thousands of charlatans before her have banked on: suggestibility and naivety."

Jordan scowled a bit at his brother's conclusion, but didn't argue.

Haven finished his pop and set the empty can aside. "What about this new claim?" he asked. "You said somebody new reported an incident."

Pierce shot his brother an uneasy glance before answering. "In my opinion? It's nothing. A group of kids cut a hole in the fence and built a bonfire in the front yard. When they got caught, one of them claimed they'd only come through the fence because they saw two girls waving them in."

"Two?" Haven asked. "Not just Cassie?"

"Two," Pierce confirmed. "Elise's ghost has been added to the mythology of the house. She's as much a legend now as Cassie was before."

"But you don't believe them?" Haven asked.

Pierce shrugged, glancing toward his brother, as if giving him permission to take over the tale. Jordan complied by answering Haven's question. "I think people are awfully quick to chalk up paranormal encounters as outright lies. Just because they were trespassing doesn't mean they didn't see anything. And just because Elise made up her history of the house doesn't mean the séance itself wasn't real."

"You think it was?" Haven asked. "You think she actually channeled somebody from the other side?"

"Damn right, I do. How else do you explain the well?"

CHAPTER 7

Twelve Years Ago

Elise didn't just scream. Her spine arched. Her head jerked back as an almost inhuman cry tore from her throat. The shriek tapered off into a strange gurgling sound, and her body seemed to convulse.

Then she went slack and silent. As quickly as it had begun, it ended. Elise sat with her head and shoulders slumped forward.

Several of them spoke at once. "Elise?" "Are you okay?" "What happened?"

For a second, there was only silence.

Elise's head came up. Her eyes were rolled back in her head, showing only the whites. And when she spoke, the low, gravelly tone didn't sound like Elise's voice at all.

"No. Not Elise."

They'd all leaned inward after Elise's scream. Now, they all sat back again, without letting go of each other's hands. They glanced around the circle at each other. Everybody looked scared, including Linsey. Haven's heart raced frantically, pounding against his ribs. Part of him still thought Elise might be playing them, but if she was, it was one hell of a trick.

"Ask her something," Pierce hissed at his brother.

Jordan turned to Elise and licked his lips. "Wh-Who are you? Are we talking to Elise?"

The answer came in the same dead, dark voice. "No. Not Elise."

"Is this Joseph?"

"Not Joseph."

"Is this Cassie?"

Elise's face twitched. Her pupils remained rolled back in her head. "Yes. Cassie."

Craig gasped. Linsey and Pierce leaned closer again, the flickering glow from the candles in the center of the circle making their faces look strangely surreal.

"Cassie," Jordan went on, "did you die here in this house?"

There was a pause before each of her answers, as if she had to dredge up each word from some deep, secret place and force it past Elise's lips. "Yes."

"Are you trapped here? Because of the murder?"

Pause. "Yes. Murder."

"Are you alone here?"

An even longer pause than before, and then, "No."

"Is Joseph here with you?"

"Girls."

"Girls?" Haven asked, barely whispering.

"Others," Elise—or maybe it really was Cassie—said. "Girls. Others."

"There are other girls in the house with you?"

"Killed."

"Joseph killed other women before he killed you?" Jordan asked.

Pause. "No." The house creaked again, the sound seeming to come from behind Haven, but he didn't turn to look. He waited for Elise to go on. "After."

"What?" Craig asked, his question seemingly directed more at the circle of friends than at Elise. "What does she mean?"

"I don't know," Linsey whispered. "How could he kill people after he was already dead?"

"Yes." There was no emotion in Elise's voice, and she didn't turn toward Linsey to answer. "Kill after."

"What girls?" Haven asked, his voice louder this time.

"Girls." With the exception of her lips and tongue, Elise was still as a piece of marble. "Work. Girls."

"Working girls?" Pierce asked. "Like…prostitutes?"

"No."

"Then what do you mean?" Jordan asked.

"Work. Girls." The voice seemed agitated now, the words coming quicker and with more urgency, although Elise didn't move. "Work. Work. Work. Girls."

Linsey gasped. "Oh my God. I think I know." She turned to Haven. "Remember the girls from the farm camp?"

"What girls?" Pierce and Jordan asked together.

They were all looking at Haven, including Linsey. It seemed it was up to him to tell this part of the story. "There are these camps of migrant farm workers, out by the orchards. Illegals. Everybody knows they're there, but that's the only way the apples get picked." American workers weren't willing to work for so little pay, and if the orchards raised their wages enough to hire legal employees, they'd have to quadruple the price of their fruit. Nobody was going to pay that much for a pound for apples, no matter how good they were. "They come and go every year, but there've been a couple of girls who went missing."

"I haven't heard about that," Pierce said.

"Not recently," Haven explained. "There was one way back, when I was a kid. And then another one four or five years ago."

"There have been a couple of others," Craig said, "but nobody knows for sure that anything bad happened."

"What do you mean?" Linsey asked.

"My dad worked some of those cases. He said half the time, the girls have just run off with one of the men and their parents don't want to admit it. They're transients. They move all over the country following the different crops." It was clear he'd heard this exact speech from his father. "There was never any proof that anything bad happened to those girls. No bodies were ever found or anything. They might have just left."

"No!" Elise snapped, making them all jump. It was almost as if they'd forgotten Elise and her trick, if that's what it was. Even Haven was beginning to have his doubts. "Girls. Girls, girls, girls!"

"Is that who you're talking about?" Jordan asked her. "The girls from the farm camp? Are they here with you?"

"Girls. Dead. Here."

"Joseph killed these working girls? I mean, uh, farm worker girls?"

The spookiest thing of all was the utterly blank expression in Elise's face. "Dead."

"This is stupid," Linsey muttered. "Elise, knock it off."

"Not. Elise!" Elise's head snapped back so hard, Haven thought he heard her neck crack. It was the first time she'd moved since Cassie—if it really was Cassie—had taken over. "Man. Kill. Girls!"

"Joseph, you mean? Joseph killed them."

"No!" Elise's head snapped back again, then forward. It was as if Cassie was gaining more control over Elise's body with each passing moment. She stared at Jordan with her spooky, rolled-back eyes. "Man! Kill!"

"Okay," Pierce said. "We believe you. But how do we prove it? What did he do with the bodies?"

Another long pause, punctuated only by the creaking house and the pounding of Haven's heart. Then, Elise said a single word.

"Well."

For a moment, there was only stunned silence as they waited for her to go on, but she didn't. "Well, what?" Jordan finally prodded.

"Bodies. Well."

"The bodies are in a well?" Haven asked. "What well?"

"Well. Here." Elise began to shake, her head jerking backward, her eyes seeming to quiver in their sockets. From the strain of keeping them rolled back in her head, or was this real? "Well. Here. Well. Here!"

"There's a well here?" Pierce prompted. "On this property?"

"That makes sense," Jordan said. "Especially given how old this house probably is, and being so far from town."

"Yes!" Elise—or whomever was speaking out of Elise's mouth—was almost shouting. "Yes! Find. Well. Here!"

Her body jerked again, convulsing backward. Her legs flew forward, knocking candles over and spilling the capful of absinthe. She was only kept upright by Jordan and Craig, who still held her hands. All the tension seemed to drain from her body at once and she slumped, falling into Jordan.

"Oh my God!" Linsey cried. "Elise!"

Their circle broke. Jordan held Elise in his arms. Craig and Linsey both let go of hands to lean across the circle toward her. The tipped candles had gone out, spilling a puddle of wax that was already beginning to harden on the cold wooden floor.

"Elise." Linsey grabbed her sister by the shoulders and shook her. "Elise, wake up!"

"Wha—?" Elise's eyelids fluttered open. She put a hand to her temple and looked around. The gesture struck Haven as somehow rehearsed, and yet she seemed genuinely confused. "What happened?"

"Are you okay?" Jordan asked.

Elise had to tip her head back to look up at him. She seemed surprised to find herself slumped across the floor, halfway in his lap. She sat up, pushing her hair off her face. "What's going on? Why are you all looking at me like that?"

"Don't you remember?" Linsey sounded like she was close to tears. "Oh my God, Elise!"

Jordan, Craig, and Linsey all started talking at once, telling her about the voice, and the bodies, and the well. Haven shifted on the hard floor, wanting to stretch his legs but not wanting to get wax all over his jeans. Haven realized Pierce still had ahold of his hand. Pierce seemed to realize it at the exact same moment.

Pierce let go of him, his cheeks turning red in the process. "Sorry."

"It's okay."

The others were beginning to sound frantic, all of them talking at once.

"Cassie said there's a well."

"Is there one on the property? Does anybody know?"

"We should tell the police!"

"They'll never believe us."

"Guys!" Elise said, loud enough to silence them all. She looked around at the circle of friends. "We have to find out."

"Right now?" Haven asked.

"Think about it. If we go to the cops, we'll just get in trouble for being in the house. What if we do that and it ends up there isn't any well at all, let alone bodies in it? We'll have gotten in trouble for nothing."

"But if there *are* bodies…" Linsey started to say.

"Exactly," Elise said, nodding. "We have to go look for the well and find out for ourselves."

"Yeah!"

"That makes sense."

"Totally."

Haven couldn't believe what he was hearing. The idea of stumbling around in the dark, looking for a well that may or may not exist, wasn't exactly how he'd hoped to spend the evening, but the others were already on their feet, looking for flashlights.

"You're serious?" Haven asked. "You want to go looking for the well right now, in the dark? Are you crazy?"

They all stared at him. Linsey was pale, her eyes wide. Craig looked determined. Pierce and Jordan were harder to read, but there was an air of tense excitement about them.

And Elise…

She almost smiled at him. He had a feeling she was about to start calling him a chicken again if he argued.

"Fine," he conceded, pushing to his feet. "Let's go find your stupid well."

CHAPTER 8

Present Day

Haven returned to his hotel room with his head spinning. Being back in that house, remembering his cousin and her wild stories...

It troubled him. And seeing Pierce again? That troubled him as well, although in a completely different way.

He was scheduled to meet Pierce and Jordan at the house the next afternoon for the on-camera interview that would be used in the beginning of the episode. Pierce had told him not to worry about it, but Haven knew having to relive that night would be unsettling.

He slept fitfully and woke with one thought on his mind—how had Elise known about the well?

If he didn't believe Jordan's premise that the message had come from beyond the grave, then where exactly had it come from? And what about Linsey's belief that there had been a secret boyfriend in Elise's life?

He debated his options as he showered and dressed but, in the end, he did what he'd known he'd do all along.

He called Pierce.

"Good morning, sunshine," Pierce said, in lieu of hello.

"I had a thought."

"Excellent. I'm a fan of thoughts. Lay it on me."

Now that he was actually talking to Pierce, Haven felt like an idiot, but it seemed too late to turn back now. He nudged his glasses back into place and dove in, giving Pierce a brief rundown of his conversation with Linsey, and her suspicion that there had been another man in her life.

Pierce was silent for a moment. Finally, he said, "Are you dressed?"

Haven blinked down at himself, a bit surprised by the question. "Yeah. Why?"

"I'll pick you up in five minutes."

It was closer to ten minutes before Pierce pulled up in a white compact car that Haven assumed was rented. Haven was glad Jordan wasn't with him.

His heart pounded a bit too hard as he climbed inside. Pierce was fresh from the shower, his hair still damp and the light smell of shampoo clinging to him. He didn't even say hi. He just angled the car onto the street, turning toward the southeast side of town.

"What's going on?" Haven asked. "You taking me out for breakfast?"

Pierce cracked a smile that didn't quite reach his eyes. "Maybe after."

"After what?"

Pierce stopped at a stop sign looking both ways before answering. "The well has always bothered me too. How in the world could Elise have known about it? Either Jordan's right, and that really was Cassie talking to us that night, or…"

He let the sentence trail off, glancing toward Haven as if asking a question. "Or," Haven said, "it was a lucky guess?"

"Maybe. Or maybe there's a possibility we hadn't thought of." He turned another corner, then pulled to the side of the road and put the car in park.

Haven looked around. They were in a residential neighborhood. Half a block up, a tiny park with a swing set and slide sat on one corner of the street.

"This is where Elise had Jordan leave her that night."

Haven fought down a surge of anger. "You mean where he claims she asked to be dropped off. Who knows where he actually dumped her after he killed her."

Pierce gripped the steering wheel hard with both hands, even though the car wasn't moving. His jaw clenched. "He didn't—"

"He was the last one to see her!"

"No. Her killer was the last one to see her."

"One and the same."

"Damn it!" Pierce smacked the steering wheel with the heel of his hand. "Is it too much to ask that you consider, just for one minute, that he might be telling the truth? I mean, Jesus, Haven. You know me!" He sighed, all of his anger seeming to drain away at once. He glanced over at Haven, his cheeks red. "You know me," he said quietly. "Maybe not well, but you do."

Haven ducked his head.

"Do you trust me," Pierce asked. "Even a little?"

"Yes." He couldn't lie about that. "I've always trusted you. It's just that—"

"I know." Pierce gripped Haven's forearm. He leaned across the center console and waited until Haven met his gaze. "I know you don't believe him. I'm not asking you to change your mind about that. Not yet, at any rate. But please, Haven. Just for the sake of the argument, can we *please* go into this assuming that my brother's telling the truth?"

Haven's heart clenched. He was sure Jordan was guilty. But at the same time, he wasn't lying. He trusted Pierce. Sitting this close to him, feeling the warmth of Pierce's hand on his arm, seeing the plea in his familiar blue eyes, Haven would have agreed to just about anything. "Okay," he relented. "For the sake of the argument, I'll agree. This is where she asked to be dropped off."

Pierce's smile was small, but grateful. "Thank you." He hesitated, almost as if he were considering leaning across the console and kissing Haven. Haven's heart burst into gear, but

Pierce only squeezed his arm once before letting go and turning back to the street.

"So," he said, his voice oddly subdued. "This is where he left her. Now...think back. Who did she know that lived in this area?"

"Only Judy Roberts." They'd been over this, years ago. "None of her other friends lived here." And Judy hadn't seen Elise at all that night.

"But Linsey suspects Elise had a boyfriend nobody knew about. And Elise told Jordan she had a friend here who would drive her home. So, whose house might she have gone to?"

They focused on the silent, empty street, thinking.

The answer came to both of them at once.

"Lance Gustafson."

"You think she was having an affair with the English teacher?" Pierce asked.

Haven shrugged. "She'd graduated the year before, so it wasn't like she was still a student." He eyed the line of houses, but he couldn't remember exactly which one had belonged to Lance. "We have to talk to him. Do you think he still lives here?"

"No." Pierce started the car and pulled out of the parking space. "He and his family left town after he was acquitted."

"I guess I can't blame him for that. There are probably plenty of people in Hobbsburg who still think he did it. So where is he now?"

"In Altoona. But he still owns the empty house in the woods, which means our producers have already contacted him. It just so happens we're scheduled to do an on-camera interview with him out there later this afternoon."

"Before or after me?"

"Before." He threw Haven a quick smile as he turned onto the main drag. "In the meantime, how about that breakfast?"

Pierce took him to the diner on Main Street. It was one they'd all hung out in as teenagers, washing down piles of French fries with whole pots of lousy coffee. The same diner where Elise had once convinced Haven and Linsey to hold a séance in a haunted house. It felt as if nothing had changed. The worn carpet, the vinyl booths, and the tired waitresses all looked exactly the same. The only thing different was that the smoking section in the back corner no longer existed, but Haven still thought he detected the odor of cigarettes, as if it lingered in the upholstery and the flowered wallpaper.

It wasn't until after they'd ordered that Haven took a minute to examine the patrons, wondering if he might recognize anybody, or if anybody would recognize him or Pierce. Pierce was obviously something of a celebrity because of the TV show, but it was on one of the smaller networks. Not exactly a prime-time hit. Besides, Pierce had only lived in Hobbsburg for a couple of years. Haven, on the other hand, had lived there for eighteen years. It seemed like there should be somebody present who knew him.

And there was.

Sergeant Fuller—except he was now *Chief* Fuller—sat with another police officer a few tables away, staring pointedly at Haven and Pierce, not bothering to hide his scowl.

"Don't look now, but Clarence Fuller's giving us the evil eye."

Pierce, of course, did what anybody would do and turned to look, despite Haven's admonition not to. Pierce threw the Chief a jaunty wave, which only made Chief Fuller scowl harder.

"What's his deal, anyway?" Haven asked, as Pierce turned back to face him.

"Well, I think I told you he didn't want us here. He assumes we'll make a big spectacle of the entire thing."

Haven wished the man weren't sitting right in his natural line of sight. It made it hard to ignore him. He looked around again, searching for familiar faces. He didn't find anybody he knew, but he did spot eight teenagers crammed into one of the big round booths in the corner, all staring pointedly in Pierce's direction.

Haven was pretty sure he'd sat in that exact same booth one of the last times he'd been here. Linsey and Craig had been arguing; Elise had been flirting with Jordan; Pierce had sat on Haven's left, his hand occasionally brushing Haven's leg. At the time, Haven had sat stock-still, his heart pounding, his cheeks on fire, wondering if the touches were intentional or accidental, practically frozen in his uncertainty. It had seemed absurd that anybody as popular as Pierce could be interested in Haven, who'd always been a bit of a bookworm.

"What's up?" Pierce asked, interrupting Haven's little stroll down memory lane.

Haven wasn't about to tell Pierce what he'd actually been thinking. Instead, he nodded toward the booth. "I think you have some fans over there."

Pierce followed his line of sight, then gave that table a wave as well. The girls giggled, and the teens immediately put their heads together to whisper excitedly.

"Does that happen a lot?" Haven asked.

"What? Being recognized as somebody on TV, you mean? Once in a while. Not as often as you might think. Sometimes they know they've seen us before, but they can't quite remember where. We get a lot of people saying stuff like, 'Hey, you were on that one episode of CSI, right?' Or, 'You're those guys who rebuild houses.'" He took a sip of coffee, eyeing Haven over the rim of the cup. "What about you? You're famous too. More than me, really. You probably get mobbed all the time."

Haven squirmed, uncomfortable with the term "famous." "Not really. Even if they read my books, most of them don't know what I look like."

"I've noticed you never have your picture on the back."

Haven unwrapped his roll of silverware, just so he could fiddle with the little paper napkin ring. He'd always been a fidgeter. Elise used to take the napkin rings away from him and stick them all together into one long chain.

Thinking about Elise made his chest ache. He wanted to drive up to her old house, to walk through the front door the way he had a thousand times as a kid. Surely he'd find her curled up on the couch, watching TV, laughing about how she'd given them all such a good scare.

Except his entire family had left Hobbsburg and moved on. It was a startling and painful realization. He thought he'd put this type of grief behind him years ago.

"I don't think I realized you and Elise were so close."

The statement startled Haven. It was almost as if Pierce had read his mind. He wasn't sure what to say. He settled for, "We were cousins."

"Well, yeah. I knew *that*. But I feel like there was some piece I was missing."

Haven folded and unfolded the little piece of paper over and over, thinking. "If you had asked me back then if we were close, I would have said no. It wasn't like we had long, intimate talks about our life goals or anything like that. But Linsey and Elise were the closest thing I had to siblings. We were always in and out of each other's houses."

"I remember you lived close to each other."

"In hindsight, it seems like we were together all the time. We'd walk up to the old high school, or downtown, or to the library. And no matter where we were or what we were doing, Elise always had a story to tell. She was always trying to convince Linsey and me that some building was haunted, or that a serial killer was lurking in the shadows, or spooky monsters were out to get us."

"Sounds like one of your books."

"It is." Haven set the little ring of paper aside to meet Pierce's eyes. "All my stories come from her."

Pierce tilted his head, a little crease forming between his eyebrows. "I'm sure the whole story doesn't, right?"

"Close enough." He might have said the next part too— the part about how he felt like a fraud for publishing them under his own name—but the waitress arrived with their food.

The next few minutes were spent in relative silence as they went to work on their breakfasts. Haven had opted for scrambled egg whites with fruit—he felt like it was all he could do these days to keep every ounce of food he ate from expanding his waistline—but Pierce had gone all in, ordering chipped beef gravy on toast and a side of pancakes. Haven couldn't help wishing he'd gone for the chipped beef gravy too. It looked a lot more appetizing than his own breakfast.

And although he didn't want to admit it, Pierce's question had taken Haven to a dark place.

Nothing had been the same after Elise's disappearance. He hadn't just lost his cousin. He'd lost his entire life. Not only was Elise gone, but Linsey had been different as well. Plus, Linsey and Elise's parents—Haven's aunt and uncle, who had always welcomed him into their home—no longer wanted him around. Even Haven's own parents had never quite looked at him the same. The picturesque perfection of his childhood had been shattered. Swept away in one horrible weekend.

"So, you live in Pittsburgh?" Pierce asked, when he was about midway through the chipped beef gravy Haven envied so much.

Haven breathed a mental sigh of relief, happy to think about the present. "Technically, I guess."

"Terrible town," Pierce said, his tone light. "I've never once met a Steelers fan who wasn't a total asshole."

"Spoken like a true Bengals fan."

"Are you saying I'm biased?"

"Are you saying you aren't?"

Pierce laughed. "Fair enough." He swapped the now-empty plate for the plate of pancakes. "So you live in Pittsburgh, but it seems like you're hardly ever there."

The frank statement surprised Haven. He sat back, eyeing Pierce.

Pierce gave him a sheepish shrug as he reached for the syrup. "I'll confess to a bit of Facebook stalking, from time to time."

Ah. That explained it. "I never even look at that. My publicist nags me to take pictures wherever I go and send them to her. She takes care of the rest." And she'd be annoyed when she found out he was spending several days with two TV celebrities and not making the most of it.

"So," Pierce prodded. "You didn't answer. Do you live in Pittsburgh or not?"

Haven laughed. "Not. Definitely not." The look in Pierce's eye told Haven he was expecting more of an answer than that. Haven pushed his empty plate aside and looked out the window at the still-familiar streets of Hobbsburg. Pittsburgh seemed light-years away. "That's where my mail goes, but I guess I'm a small-town boy at heart, you know? I never feel at home in the city."

"So you travel a lot."

It was more statement than question, and Haven nodded. "I do. One of the benefits of the job, I guess. I can work anywhere." He waited as the waitress refilled his coffee, then leaned his elbows on the table. "What about you?"

"The same, really. My parents are back in Ohio now. I was there for a while. I've been in Philly the last few years, but I've never learned to say 'soda' instead of 'pop.'" He shrugged. "I'm like you in that regard, I guess. I'd rather be in a place where driving across town isn't an all-day event."

"So why stay?"

"That's where Jordan lives." He'd nearly finished the pancakes. God knew how he could eat like that and still look as good as he did. "He had a girlfriend there. Pretty serious too. I thought she'd be the one. But they broke up a couple of months ago, so he'll probably pack up and move to Columbus or Jersey or Buffalo. Some other damned place I can't stand to be in."

"So why stay with him?"

"Because he's my brother. Why else?" He didn't wait for Haven to answer. "Anyway, the job keeps us moving. When we aren't filming, we do our own private investigations on the side. Sometimes it feels like we're in a new town every week, which suits me just fine." There was a note of sadness in his voice, and Haven realized the slight emphasis on "me" in the last sentence.

"But not Jordan?"

Pierce frowned. "That's the main reason he and his girlfriend broke up—because he was always gone. She didn't trust him to stay faithful."

"Did he?"

Pierce squinted at him and crossed his arms over his chest. "Still determined to think the worst of him, aren't you?"

Haven was relieved when they were suddenly interrupted. "Excuse me? Are you one of the *Paranormal Hunters*?" They turned to find three of the teenagers who'd been watching them standing a foot away. Two males—one tall with black hair, one short and blond—plus one female, sporting a nose ring. It was the latter who'd spoken.

Pierce gave them a dazzling smile, his annoyance at Haven apparently forgotten. "I am."

"Can we get your autograph?"

"Of course. What do you want me to sign?"

The kids all looked at each other, clearly having not thought this far ahead.

"Here." Pierce took his paper placemat and folded it into quarters, then unfolded it and began tearing it along the lines. "You guys know Haven Sage, right?" His hands were occupied, but he sort of nodded in Haven's direction. "He's a famous horror author. He grew up here."

The girl and the taller of the two boys looked mightily unimpressed, but the smaller of the boys broke into a broad smile. "I know you! You wrote that book about the haunted boarding school."

"I did. It was sort of based on the old high school here in Hobbsburg. The empty one up on Eighth Street?"

"Oh my God, I could totally see that. That building's spooky."

"Is it still there?"

He nodded. "They keep talking about tearing it down, but they haven't yet." He turned to his friends. "You guys should really read his book. It was like, this school for troubled kids and stuff, but it was haunted, because it'd been an asylum in the old days, and then all this crazy shit starts happening, man. All the students and the teachers start acting weird, and then—"

His friends were clearly far more interested in talking to Pierce than in listening to their friend recap a boring old book. "Are you here for an investigation?" Nose Ring asked.

"It must be the old Gustafson manor, outside of town," the taller of the boys said. "The one with the chain-link fence around it?"

Pierce was in the middle of signing one of the placement fragments, but he glanced up at Haven with a grin. "'Manor'? I kind of like the sound of that."

Now that it was clear they were welcome, the teens' friends came to wait their turn for an autograph. Haven went to work tearing his own paper placemat into quarters. The teens were all talking at once.

"So you're investigating the Gustafson house?"

"Is the lockdown tonight?"

"Have you seen anything yet?"

Pierce held up a hand. "I'm not really supposed to tell you where we're—"

"What's going on here?"

If he hadn't been so focused on tearing up his placemat for Pierce's fans, Haven might have seen Chief Fuller approaching. As it was, he was as surprised as anyone when the man pushed his way to the center of the group, eyeing all the kids as if he'd caught them painting graffiti on his favorite church.

"All of you, quit making pests of yourselves. Go back to your table." He turned to glare on Pierce. "I told you not to make a scene, and what do you do? You show up in the middle of breakfast and hold an autograph session."

Pierce's smile stayed in place, but Haven noted a little pin scratch of annoyance between Pierce's brows. "We were only having breakfast. We didn't mean to cause a scene."

The teens glowered at the Chief, but didn't say anything. They hung back—not quite returning to their table, but trying to put a bit of distance between them and Chief Fuller anyway. Haven sympathized. They hadn't been doing anything wrong, but Fuller was acting like they were all delinquents.

Pierce pointedly finished the autograph he'd been working on and stretched past the scowling police chief to hand it to its intended recipient. "All finished," he said to Chief Fuller with a smile. "No harm done, right?"

The waitress appeared at the Chief's elbow, although she barely spared him a glance. "Is there a problem?" she asked Pierce.

"No," Pierce said, still smiling. "But since you're here, I guess it's time for the check."

The waitress complied. The teens and Chief Fuller returned to their respective tables. Nobody but Chief Fuller had noticed Haven and Pierce come in, but Haven was pretty sure every eye in the restaurant watched them leave.

Later that day, Pierce once again picked Haven up from his motel, although, this time, Jordan was driving. Pierce sat in the passenger seat. Haven climbed in behind them, feeling a strange sense of déjà vu as they headed out of town, toward the Gustafson house.

Pierce turned halfway around in his seat in order to more easily talk to Haven. "Lance didn't want to talk to us at first. He's pretty determined to pretend nothing strange ever happened out here at all."

"He clearly agreed eventually."

"He did, but certain topics are off limits."

"The well?" Haven guessed.

Jordan laughed. "Got it in one."

"The well and anything having to do with his trial," Pierce continued. "He might not have much to say, to be honest. But if you've seen the show, you know how much Jeremy likes to open with interviews of witnesses in front of the property in question."

"Witnesses? Did Lance actually witness anything?" Haven asked.

Pierce shrugged. "I guess we'll find out."

They made the rest of the drive in silence, finally entering the gated property and parking next to the *Paranormal Hunters* production truck. Lance Gustafson stood next to a battered green Volvo station wagon, waiting for them.

He hadn't aged well. He was rail-thin and pasty-white, with a badly receding hairline. He shook hands with Pierce and Jordan, but balked when he saw Haven standing behind them.

"You didn't say anything about him being here."

"He won't be part of the interview," Pierce said. He threw Haven a pleading glance, seemingly asking him to not to disagree.

"I'll wait by the cars," Haven said, and smiled when Pierce mouthed a "thank you" in his direction.

Haven watched from a distance as the interview went down. It was a format he'd seen on many of the *Paranormal Hunters* episodes, although he'd certainly never seen the behind-the-scenes version. Todd held the camera. Pierce had the manila folder full of research and photos under one arm. Justine waited off to the side, ready to rearrange their hair or dust their faces with powder between takes. Jeremy stood behind the cameraman, occasionally stopping the shoot to have them ask a question again, but in a different way.

The brothers started out with the story of how Lance—although they always called him "Mr. Gustafson"—had once been their high school English teacher. After that, Lance was asked to give a brief history of the house. His version was about halfway between the scrubbed-down "official" version and the far-fetched tale Elise had once told her friends. Pierce and Jordan asked questions as he talked, leading him through the story. Pierce occasionally showed Lance photos from the folder. Lance became visibly shaken when it came time to talk about his brother's suicide. The picture of Joseph brought tears to his eyes. But when asked about paranormal encounters, his answer was surprisingly boring.

"I've never seen or heard anything unusual out here." He glanced over at the house and frowned. "Then again, I never come here. I don't even have a key to the gate. The last time I was here was twelve years ago, when the— When—" He ducked his head and covered his eyes.

"When our friend Elise went missing?" Pierce asked.

Lance nodded. "Yes." His voice shook, and when Pierce tried to hand him another photo—Haven assumed it was of Elise—Lance turned away without taking it. "Excuse me. I need a minute."

The director signaled to the cameraman to stop filming. Several minutes went by before Lance regained his composure. Haven wondered what exactly had shaken him so much. Was it his brother's suicide, or remembering the crimes he himself had been charged with, or seeing Elise's smiling face? Or was it because he was to blame for Elise's disappearance?

Finally, the camera started rolling again. Pierce and Jordan asked a few more questions about the ongoing rumors and the latest incident, but Lance had nothing more of interest to contribute. Even knowing zilch about TV production, Haven knew those last few questions and answers would never make it to the final episode.

Jeremy finally ended the interview, and the brothers exchanged a glance. They'd obviously arranged this part between them in advance. Jordan easily maneuvered the crew back into the house, leaving Lance alone with Pierce and Haven.

"Now, Mr. Gustafson," Pierce said, as Haven approached. "Haven and I have a few more question for you."

Lance took a step backward, his eyes on Haven. "I've already told you everything I know—"

"I don't think you have," Haven said.

Lance ducked his head to stare nervously at his toes.

"My cousin Linsey has a theory," Haven said. "She thinks Elise was seeing somebody when she disappeared."

Lance glanced uneasily at Pierce. "Well, yeah. She was seeing Jordan, right?"

Pierce shook his head. "Not really."

"According to Linsey," Haven said, "Elise had been seeing somebody for at least a few weeks, but it was somebody she felt she needed to keep secret."

"She had my brother drop her off by your house that night," Pierce said. "At the time, nobody knew why she picked that street. Everybody assumed she was going to Judy Roberts's house, but Judy never saw her. So the question is, who else might she have planned to see?"

"Stop. Please. My family—"

But Haven interrupted, wanting to push their advantage. "You lied about it back then, because you didn't want your wife to find out. But it was you, wasn't it? You were the secret boyfriend."

Lance put his face in his hands, his shoulders shaking.

"You couldn't even look at her photo just now," Haven said. "Now tell me truth. Was it you? Were you the 'friend' she told Jordan would drive her home?"

It took Lance a second to answer. "Yes," he finally whispered. "We'd been seeing each other for almost two months."

Haven's heart burst into gear. Finally, they were going to get some real answers about that night. "Did you see her that night?"

"I didn't kill her! I didn't do anything to her!"

"But *did you see her*?"

He nodded, dropping his hands. "Yes." He sounded shaken, but Haven noticed that despite his emotional display a moment before, his eyes were completely dry. "I saw her."

"Tell us," Pierce said.

Lance shook his head, stricken. "My wife— After everything that's happened, she'd never forgive me!"

"If what you say is true," Haven said, "if you didn't hurt Elise, then your wife never has to know." He wasn't sure it was a promise he could keep, but it was one he was willing to make, if it got Lance talking.

Lance glanced wildly around them, eyeing the house. Pierce seemed to guess what was troubling him. "There are no hidden cameras," he promised, his voice low. "We're not trying to trick you. This has nothing to do with the TV show. We just want to know what happened that night."

"This won't go on air? Can you promise me it won't be on TV?"

"We promise," Haven and Pierce said in unison.

Lance rubbed his forehead, as if he could massage away his worry lines. After a moment of silent debate, he started to speak. "My wife always went to bed early, because she worked the 5:00 A.M. shift. After she and the kids were in bed, I'd grade papers in my study. Elise would just...show up. There was a French door from my study onto the back patio, and she'd come by and tap on the glass. And...I'd let her in."

"That's what happened that night?" Haven asked.

Lance nodded. "I was surprised to see her, because she'd told me she had plans with her cousins. But then she said she'd had an argument with somebody there, and she wanted to see me."

"What happened after that?" Pierce asked.

Lance looked up at the sky, his cheeks turning red. "We, uh…well…"

"Okay," Haven said. "I think we can guess what happened next." Although seeing the way Lance had ended up, it turned Haven's stomach to think of him with Elise. But Lance had been twelve years younger back then, and far less broken. "Tell us what happened after *that*."

"She wanted me to drive her home, but I couldn't."

"Why not?"

"The master bedroom was right over the garage. There was no way I could leave in the car without Kathy finding out."

"And because of that, Elise never made it home," Haven said, his voice rising in anger. "You couldn't have just made up some story? You couldn't have just told your wife you had a sudden craving for rocky road ice cream or something?"

Lance shoved his hands deep in his pants pockets. "I didn't think of that, okay? Elise asked me to drive her home, and I said I couldn't. She said to forget it, it wasn't that far to walk anyway. I didn't know—" He held up both hands, taking another step backwards. "I had no way of knowing what would happen."

"What about when the cops came to talk to you?" Haven asked. "Did you even *once* think about telling the truth?"

"I thought about it, yes. But she was only at my house for twenty minutes or so. Thirty, max. Then she left. I didn't see how it could matter, either way."

"What about the key to this house?" Pierce asked. "Did you give her that?"

"No. She must have stolen it off my key ring at some point." He shook his head, turning to look at the house. "She asked me a lot of questions about this place when we first started seeing each other. She had sort of a morbid fascination with it."

"She loved spooky things," Haven said.

Lance nodded. "I guess that was it. She was always asking questions about Joseph, and Cassie Kennedy, and whether or not I really thought he was a killer. She asked me multiple times to bring her here, but I never did. I finally told her to drop it. My brother died here. I know everybody else remembers him as some kind of deranged killer, but I never thought of him that way. He was my hero."

"Your *hero*?" Haven couldn't hide his astonishment.

"He was my big brother." Lance turned to Pierce. "You understand, right? You understand how they'll always be a brother first, no matter what?"

Pierce looked shaken at having Jordan compared to Joseph, but he nodded. "Of course."

"This house," Lance went on. "It's not a happy place for me. It wasn't something I wanted to dwell on. I told her I never wanted to talk about it again." He turned back to face them with a shrug. He seemed more at ease, now that the truth was out. "She did as I asked. I thought she'd forgotten about it."

"You didn't know she'd been here that night?"

"Not until later, no. Not until the police came to my house, asking about the key."

"You told them you'd lost it," Haven said.

Lance nodded. "It had always been on my key ring. When Chief Daavettila asked me to get it…well, that's when I realized it was gone. She must have taken it off my key ring at some point. Saying I'd lost it seemed true enough at the time."

Jordan and Jeremy emerged from the house, laughing together at something, but when Jeremy wasn't looking, Jordan gave Pierce a "hurry up" gesture. It seemed they were out of time.

Haven and Pierce eyed each other, each of them seeming to ask if the other could think of any more questions for Lance. It was Pierce who finally broke the silence.

"So you have no idea where Elise went after she left your house?"

"I assumed she went home." He sighed, and for the first time since their arrival, he met Haven's gaze. "I should have told the truth. I know that. But it was more than just my family at stake. It was my job too. I would have been fired if anybody found out I was sleeping with a nineteen-year-old former student. But I swear to you, I didn't hurt her. I... I loved her. There's nobody who wants to see her killer caught more than me."

CHAPTER 9

Twelve Years Ago

Elise wasn't a bad person. Haven knew that. Over the years, he'd spent more hours with her and Linsey than he could count. They'd grown up only a block away from each other. He'd spent as much time at their house as he had at his own.

Elise always liked her tall tales. That much was true. But she knew when to back off. When they were kids, she'd always managed to end the game before Linsey or Haven got too scared and went running for an adult. It wasn't that she was cruel or vindictive. She just had a strange affinity for making up outlandish tales and seeing how far she could take them.

Once, when Haven was only seven or eight years old, Elise had tried to convince him and Linsey that the house behind hers was a halfway home for dangerous criminals. When Haven had asked why he'd never heard this story before, she'd informed him that the adults wanted to keep it a secret, so as not to alarm the kids, but she'd overheard her parents talking about it.

"But they could come to our house anytime!" Linsey had cried. "They could rob us or kill us or—"

"No," Elise had assured her. "There's an invisible force field between our house and theirs. Haven't you ever noticed how the rabbits can get through, but the dogs can't? That's because it's like a chain-link fence, only invisible. There are gaps in it big enough for rabbits and birds, but if you try to walk through it, it'll shock you so bad you'll pass out."

"Nu-uh." Haven had been incredulous. "There's no such thing as an invisible force field." But he hadn't been brave enough to walk over and stick his arm through to prove her wrong.

"Watch," Elise had said. "I'll show you."

She'd spent the next half hour throwing rocks at the supposed force field, waiting for one to bounce off.

Of course, none of them had. Each one had flown through the space to land in the adjacent back yard. Haven had never been exactly sure what she'd expected to happen, but she'd continued throwing rocks, encouraging them to try too, until Linsey and Haven had grown bored with the game and gone inside to watch TV.

A few weeks later, when Haven had finally worked up the nerve to try walking through Elise's force field, she hadn't even batted an eye before calmly explaining that the force field was gone because the criminals had been moved to a new location a few days before.

Haven pondered this as the group prepared to go stumbling around in the dark looking for a well that probably didn't even exist.

"I need to pee before we go," Linsey groaned.

She wasn't the only one.

Haven had a feeling Elise was frustrated at losing the momentum she'd built up, but she was outvoted.

They split into two groups. The boys lined up on the front porch to urinate over the railing, while Linsey and Elise went around the far side of the house to squat in the tall grass.

It was cooler outside than they'd anticipated. Once back inside, they donned sweatshirts and jackets. Craig drank a bit more of the absinthe. Jordan and Pierce decided to break into the beer. Haven gulped down half a can of pop.

"Come on, you guys," Elise prodded, when it looked like they might back out and spend the rest of the night drinking instead. "We don't have all night."

Technically, they *did* have all night. It was dark outside, but it was only a little past ten. Still, Haven didn't bother contradicting her.

"It's probably behind the house," Elise said. "They would have picked a place that was easy to get to from the kitchen."

That made sense to the rest of them, so they followed her through the kitchen and out the back door.

Logically, Haven knew it couldn't be darker in the back yard than the front, but it sure seemed that way. He glanced up at the sky, looking for the moon. He found only a vast field of stars.

"Shit!" Pierce swore behind him. "My batteries must be dead."

"You put new ones in it right before we left the house." Jordan turned the beam of his own flashlight onto his brother. "They can't be dead."

"They shouldn't be, but they are." Pierce slapped the flashlight against his palm a couple of times before flicking the switch again, but the light didn't come on.

"Mine's dead too," Craig said.

"Spirits can drain batteries," Elise said. "I read that on the Internet. They use the electricity to manifest. I bet Cassie tapped into the flashlight batteries while she was talking to us."

"Or you took their batteries out while we weren't looking," Haven said.

"When would I have done that?" she asked.

"The batteries are still in it," Pierce said, interrupting the argument before it could begin. "They're just dead."

"Mine too," Craig said. Linsey shone her light on him. He'd taken the top off the flashlight. He tipped it show them the silver end of the battery inside the handle.

"We still have four working lights," Elise said. "It'll have to do."

"Yours still works, Haven?" Pierce asked.

Haven's flashlight was small enough to fit in his coat pocket. He pulled it out and was relieved when it flared to life. "Looks like it." Which meant Elise was right—they had four working lights. Was he the only one who realized she'd already known his batteries weren't dead? Because his light had been in his pocket when she'd gotten ahold of the others?

"It's creepy out here," Linsey said, shining her light around them. It didn't reach far. She jerked it back and forth, trying to focus on something. It only served to accentuate the shadows between the many trees, making Haven realize how little they could actually see.

Elise swung the other way, whipping her light around. "What was that?"

"What was what?" Craig asked.

"Didn't you hear that?"

A twig snapped off to their right. They all turned their lights that direction, but found only trees.

"There's someone out here," Elise hissed.

"It's just a deer," Haven said. "Or a raccoon."

"It wasn't a deer. I'm telling you…"

"What if she's right?" Linsey asked. "What if we aren't alone? What if Joseph comes for us, just like he did for those farm girls?"

Haven shook his head in exasperation. "Look, you guys are the ones who wanted to do this. Are we going to look for the well or not?"

"He's right," Elise said. Of course. She wanted them scared. She wasn't going to let them all return to the house now, not when there were still so many hours of fun to be had. "As long as we stay together"—she put just the right amount of fear mixed with determination into her voice—"we'll probably be okay." She bit her lip. "Probably."

"Where should we start?" Jordan asked.

"I don't know. Back here, maybe?" She shined her light off to their left. The clearing extended a bit farther on that side, the ring of trees that surrounded them a bit more distant.

"Sure, let's try that."

Elise and Jordan took the lead, with Linsey and Craig behind them. Linsey jumped every time a leaf rustled or a twig snapped. The beam of her flashlight jerked from side to side as she walked. She was obviously scared, but Craig seemed determined to help Elise find the well.

Pierce fell into the rear with Haven. He stuffed his hands into the front pocket of his Cincinnati Bengals hoodie, glancing nervously around at the dark woods. "I'll just stick with you, if that's okay," he said quietly.

Haven's heart skipped a beat. He bit back a smile. "Of course."

"I mean, I promised Jordan I'd stay out of his way tonight. And, to tell you the truth, Elise is creeping me out."

"Don't let her get to you." Haven thought again about the ridiculous force field, and all the rocks she'd thrown that day, even though she had to know they'd never bounce back at her. "She just likes to mess with people."

"Yeah, but..." It took a second for Pierce to decide how to proceed. "That seemed pretty serious back there in the house, didn't it?" He shuddered. "How could she roll her eyes back like that? You don't think that was real?"

Haven remembered his own doubts during the séance. Elise's eyes had been awfully spooky. "I don't know."

"Have you ever seen her do that before? Or heard her talk like that?"

A cold shiver worked its way down Haven's spine as he remembered the flat, gravelly voice that had come out of Elise's mouth. "No."

They took a few steps in silence. Then Pierce asked another question. "What if there really are bodies? What will that mean?"

Haven shook his head. "I don't know about that either."

CHAPTER 10

Present Day

Once Lance was gone, it was Haven's turn in front of the camera.

"Forget everything I told you yesterday," Pierce said, before they started filming. "We're going to ask about that night, and I want you to answer as if everything Elise said was true."

"So you want me to lie?"

"No," Jordan said. "We want you to tell the truth as it was for you back then."

Haven's instinct was to scowl at him, or argue. Pierce seemed to sense Haven's hostility. He stepped between them, putting his hand on Haven's elbow, forcing Haven to meet his eyes. "Just remember, we're talking about what we *thought* we knew as teenagers, not what we know now. Understand?"

Haven nodded, trying to focus his attention on the looming lens of the camera. "Yeah, I get it."

"We're going to talk about Elise. Are you okay with that?"

Haven's stomach clenched at the thought, but he nodded. "Yes."

"Good. Jordan's going to focus on the séance and the possible haunting. He's going to play up the supernatural side of it."

"But—"

"I know you don't believe it. That isn't the point."

"The truth isn't the point?"

"Not yet, no." He smiled at Haven, although he let go of his arm at the same time. "You've seen the show, right?" He moved to the side, turning toward his brother, somehow allowing him back into their conversation. "Jordan's the believer. I'm the skeptic. Those are the roles we play."

"Ah." Haven nodded, finally understanding, as he considered the format of the show. The people the brothers talked to before beginning their "investigation" always came off a bit wacky. "All these interviews are intentionally tilted Jordan's way, to make the house seem spookier."

Jordan smiled at him, looking so much like his brother that Haven found it disconcerting. "It's entertainment. Mystery is far more interesting than facts."

"We're good to roll," Todd said, hefting his camera onto his shoulder. Jeremy stood at his side, the same folder tucked under his arm. "Let us know when you're ready."

Both brothers looked at Haven.

He was nervous, but not overly so. His nose had been powdered by Justine. She stepped up to do it again, making him wonder if he was extra shiny. "Let's get it over with," he said when she finished.

Despite having said they were "good to roll," it still took several minutes of testing, moving to various spots outside the house to check light levels and framing. The wind had picked up a bit, blowing all of their hair into their faces.

"Forget it," the director finally said. "Let's do it inside."

They tramped up the stairs and through the front door of the house. It wasn't as bad now, entering it for the second time in two days, especially with the sun still shining outside and the *Paranormal Hunters* crew at his heels. After what seemed like a ridiculous amount of debate, they decided to do the interview in the living room, where they'd held the original séance. Several minutes were again spent getting the lighting just right, until finally, they began.

"We're standing inside the mysterious Gustafson manor," Jordan began, "with horror author Haven Sage. It's good to have you with us, Haven. We're all big fans of your books."

Haven tried not to squirm. He also tried not to laugh at hearing the dumpy old house described as a "manor." He couldn't help glancing at Pierce, who had obviously told Jordan about the kids at the diner. Pierce winked at him. Haven had to tear his eyes away and force himself to answer Jordan's question. "Uh...thanks. Yeah. It's good to be here." He wanted to slap himself immediately. What a ridiculous thing to say! It was good to be in the place where his cousin had gone missing? Neither Jordan or Pierce seemed to notice.

"Haven was with us on that fateful night when we first entered this house and felt its dark energy." Haven was glad he'd seen Lance's interview, because it meant he wasn't surprised when Pierce shoved a picture of Elise into his hands.

It was her senior photo—the classic "lean against the tree" pose. She looked as beautiful as ever, her almost-black hair shining in the sunlight, her eyes bright and full of laughter.

"Haven," Jordan went on, "your cousin Elise was the one who came up with the idea of spending the night in this house. Why do you think she did that?"

Haven blinked, thrown a bit off foot. He'd expected to start with a mundane recap of the night's events, not a dissection of Elise's motives. "Elise loved spooky things. Any time we rented movies, she went straight for the horror section. Every Halloween she dragged us through the haunted house attractions as many times as she could. She just seemed to have a fascination with fear."

"So she found the supernatural intriguing?" Jordan asked.

"Well..." Haven didn't think that was what he'd said. Not really, at any rate, but Jordan was already pressing on.

"That night, Elise led us in a séance." He held his hands out, palm down, indicating the bare wooden floor, where they'd once sat in a circle together. "Right here, in this very spot, Elise attempted to contact the spirits of Cassie Kennedy or her killer, Joseph Gustafson."

"Yes, that's right."

Pierce took over. "Why don't you describe for us, in your own words, what happened during that séance."

It was harder to talk about than he expected. Lord knew he'd been over it in his head a thousand times the past twelve years. But somehow, recounting it out loud, the strange terror of that night came back to him in a way it never had before. Maybe it was the oddly familiar echo of the wind outside, and the creak of the house around them. Maybe it was having Pierce and Jordan next to him, just as they had been that night. Whatever the reason, by the time he got to the declarations about the well, his heart was pounding and his hands shaking.

"And that," Jordan said to the camera, "would end up being one of the biggest mysteries of that night, and of this haunted property. Who told Elise about the well?"

Haven shook his head. "I have no idea."

Pierce handed Haven another picture from his folder, one Haven had never seen before. It was an old black-and-white photo, stiff and cracked around the edges. It showed a well, complete with a little wooden roof, a hand crank, and a bucket hanging from a chain. The light came from behind the well, somehow highlighting how isolated it was, even though the woods grew thick around it.

"Is this it?" Haven asked, stunned.

"Taken when the house was first built," Jordan said. "Crazy, isn't it?"

Haven nodded. It seemed so innocent, like the wishing well in the center of town he'd tossed pennies into as a kid. There was nothing to hint at the horror it would later hold. "If it'd looked like this twelve years ago, we wouldn't have had such a hard time finding it." He handed it back to Pierce, feeling somehow tainted for having held it at all.

"Now, Haven," Pierce said. The cameraman shifted a bit to one side, seemingly to better fit them all in the picture again. "You knew your cousin better than any of us. You've told us since then that she had a flare for the theatrical. But before that night, had you ever heard your cousin speak in that voice?"

Pierce knew his answer already because it was the same one he'd given him that night, as they hunted for the well. "No."

"Had you ever seen her roll her eyes back in her head like that?"

"No."

"Do you think it could have all been an act?"

"Well—"

"Or," Jordan interrupted, "do you think it's possible she truly channeled the spirit of Cassie Kennedy?"

Haven swallowed, his throat so dry, it felt like sandpaper. "I can't explain what happened."

The brothers exchanged a glance, as if considering whose turn it was to speak. After a moment of wordless consultation, Pierce picked up the questioning. "Haven…" And Haven could tell just from his tone that he was afraid to ask. "Let me ask you this. What do you think happened to Elise that night?"

Haven's eyes flew to Jordan, but Pierce kept talking, not letting Haven answer just yet.

"What I mean is, that was the last time anybody saw her, but a lot of folks around here think she ran away. What do you think about that theory? Do you think she's still alive out there somewhere?"

Haven shook his head, fighting a sudden lump in his throat. "No."

They waited for him to say more, but he had nothing else to add.

"You think she died that night, one way or another?" Pierce asked, his voice gentle.

Haven nodded. "She must have."

"Because of this house?" Jordan asked.

"No." Haven glanced around the room, noting the stain where the candle had spilled its wax, and the spot Elise had claimed was Cassie's blood. He turned to eye the banister where Joseph Gustafson had committed suicide. He considered Lance Gustafson's admission that he'd seen Elise after Jordan dropped her off. "I don't know."

"If Elise really did die that night," Jordan said, "do you think she could still be still here? Do you think it's possible she now haunts this house, alongside Cassie and Joseph and whatever other spirits might be trapped here?"

Haven's gut reaction was one of derision. Of course Elise wasn't haunting the Gustafson house. But his urge to scoff at Jordan changed to amusement as he remembered the stories Elise had told him through his youth. Her laundry room being possessed. The back of her closet hiding a portal to hell. The old high school, sitting abandoned in the middle of town, having once been an insane asylum, the spirits of its inmates still roaming the halls.

"Well," he said at last, surprised at his own urge to laugh, "if she is here, I imagine she's looking forward to having you in the house again. I bet she has all kinds of things in store for you."

Again, the brothers exchanged glances, but this time, Haven had the distinct feeling they were pleased with his answer.

"Tell us what you mean," Jordan said, his eyes bright with eagerness. "Are you saying she'll be out to get us?"

"No. At least, not the way you mean. Elise wouldn't ever be violent. But the thing is, scaring the wits out of people was her favorite thing in the world. I can't imagine something as simple as death could ever change that."

CHAPTER 11

Twelve Years Ago

They couldn't find the well.

They spent over an hour wandering around in the woods, looking for it. Elise did her best to keep them scared. She jumped at every sound, claimed to hear footsteps of somebody following them, and swore on multiple occasions that she'd seen something hiding in the trees.

"It's probably Joseph's ghost," she said, gripping Jordan's arm. "He's trying to stop us from finding the well."

It was a show-stopping performance, but the climax had come and gone. There was just no way to maintain that level of tension for so long. Haven's feet and legs ached. His right hand—the one in his coat pocket—was warm enough, but the one holding the flashlight was freezing.

"This is stupid," he muttered to Pierce, as they tramped through the trees. "I say we go back."

"Good idea," Pierce replied. "I'll come with you."

Haven smiled, secretly pleased, his weariness forgotten.

"Haven's right," Craig said, slurring his words. "We can look more in the morning."

"I think we should keep looking," Elise said. She turned to Jordan. "You'll stay with me, right?"

Jordan appeared torn. He clearly didn't want to keep wandering through the woods in the dark, but he was doing everything he could to impress Elise. "Sure," he said at last. "We may as well finish what we started. There aren't that many places left to look."

Haven, Pierce, Craig, and Linsey left them to it and turned back to the house. They'd wandered deep into the thick woods. The house was farther away than Haven realized. Craig staggered a bit as they walked. Linsey still jumped every time a twig cracked.

Finally they climbed the steps and went through the back door of the house, into the kitchen. It was pitch black inside. Haven played his flashlight over the empty countertops. The house creaked again, and Haven stopped in his tracks. Whether the séance had been real or not, Haven didn't know, but the house was creepy. Suddenly, following Elise through the woods didn't seem so bad.

Linsey and Craig went up the stairs to their room.

Pierce gestured up the stairs, meeting Haven's eyes with an intensity that unnerved him. "After you."

Haven gulped, his stomach such a mess of nerves and excitement, he worried he'd be sick before he reached the top. Pierce followed him up the stairs, so close he was practically treading on Haven's heels. Haven didn't know which scared him more—the house or facing the next few minutes.

Once in the small bedroom they'd chosen, Haven pulled out his sleeping bag and spread it on the floor. The innocent simplicity of the action calmed him, and he was pleased when Pierce unrolled his own bag right alongside, only an inch or two of floor between them. The moon had come up as they'd searched for the well. It was only half full, casting a bit of light through the window. At least it wasn't as dark as it had been downstairs.

They kicked off their sneakers and shed their jackets, but otherwise remained dressed. It was chilly in the room, although not as bad as it had been outside. Haven knew he'd be warm enough once he was in his sleeping bag.

"That was pretty crazy, wasn't it?" Pierce asked, sitting cross-legged on his bag across from Haven.

"Elise keeps things interesting."

"Yeah but... I don't know if she could have faked that Cassie thing. And what about the flashlights?"

It was a fair question. "You definitely put in new batteries before you left home?"

"Positive."

"Let me see it."

Haven handed his own flashlight to Pierce and had him aim the beam so he could see what he was doing. He could tell just by hefting Pierce's flashlight that it had batteries in it. Once he opened the top and spilled them out into his hands, he saw the problem.

"She flipped one around," he said, holding it out for Pierce to see. "The top battery is in backwards."

"It wasn't, though. It was working before—"

"I know."

"You're saying Elise did it?"

"It's the most likely explanation."

"When?"

"I don't know. While we were peeing? Or maybe when we were scoping out the rooms. You didn't have your light with you then, and she was already setting up for the séance when we went back down."

Pierce shook his head, chuckling. "Man. She really had me going."

"It's what she does best."

For a moment, they sat there in silence, suddenly awkward and unsure. Then they heard a low moan from the room next door.

"I guess we know what they're doing," Haven said. He flipped off his flashlight so Pierce wouldn't see the way it made him blush.

"I guess." Pierce seemed as uncomfortable as Haven felt. "So what should we do? Any ideas? I mean, I don't know about you, but I'm not sure I can sleep right now."

Haven's heart raced, pounding so hard in his chest that it took his breath away. This was it. This was exactly what he'd hoped for. But did he have enough nerve to say what was on his mind?

There was a chance Pierce would freak out, or laugh at him, or even fly off the handle at the suggestion. But Haven didn't think any of those things would happen. They'd been acquaintances since the Hunter family had moved to Hobbsburg two years earlier. They'd started hanging out more the previous spring. But something had definitely changed between them in the last few weeks. Every time they were together, Haven felt Pierce's eyes on him. He noticed the way Pierce seemed to move closer to him, and the way the older boy seemed to find excuses to touch him.

Haven cleared his throat and took a deep breath. "We could—" His voice was so quiet, Pierce had to lean a bit closer to hear. Haven had to stop and steady himself. "We could, you know…do the same thing."

He waited, his pulse pounding in his ears, for Pierce's reaction. He wished there was a bit more light in the room so he could see his face.

"Well," Pierce said. "I don't think we could do *exactly* what they're doing."

His tone was gentle. He was teasing, but not mocking.

Still, Haven's cheeks burned even hotter. "No, not exactly." He hadn't really meant sex, per se. Just a bit of normal teenage exploration. "I just thought maybe…"

"Maybe what?" Pierce prompted.

Haven had to grip his hands together to keep them from shaking. But Pierce hadn't flat-out said no, so he pressed on. "Kissing?"

Pierce was quiet for a moment, and Haven waited for what would come next. "Is that what you want?" Pierce finally asked, his voice a whisper. "For me to kiss you?"

Haven couldn't speak. He could only nod, hoping Pierce could see him in the near darkness.

Pierce glanced toward the open bedroom door. "Do you think there's a lock on that?"

The sudden rush of relief and excitement left Haven lightheaded. "I can find out."

His knees felt like rubber as he crossed the room to close the door. He turned the lock in the center of the knob. It wouldn't keep Michael Myers or Jason Voorhees at bay, but it'd be enough to keep Jordan or Elise from walking in on them. He turned back to the sleeping bags, suddenly afraid of what came next.

"Well," Pierce said at last. "I can't kiss you if you're all the way over there."

Haven took off his glasses first, leaving them on top of his backpack. He wanted to be able to find them easily later, but he had a feeling they'd be in the way if he left them on his face.

It was only a guess. He had zero experience with this kind of thing.

He returned to his spot across from Pierce and sat cross-legged on his sleeping bag. The inch or two of floor space between the bags suddenly seemed insurmountable, like the most treacherous abyss he'd ever imagined.

Luckily, Pierce had no problem leaning across that chasm.

Sometime later, when they were both breathless and wonderfully tangled in each other's limbs, their clothes still on, but not quite the way they were supposed to be, Pierce whispered in Haven's ear. "I want you to know, you're the only reason I came on this stupid trip."

Haven smiled, loving the feel of Pierce's weight on top of him, the way Pierce's hands seemed to be everywhere at the same time. There was one question he wanted to ask. "Do you like girls too?"

Pierce pulled back a bit, as if to see Haven's face in the dim light. "Does it matter?"

"Not really, I guess. I'm just curious."

Pierce chuckled. He brushed his lips up the side of Haven's neck, sending a delicious shiver down his spine. "My brother likes girls enough for both of us."

CHAPTER 12

Present Day

"You gave us some great answers back there," Pierce said as he drove Haven back to his hotel. Jordan wasn't with them. A second *Paranormal Hunters* truck full of people and gear had arrived just as they were preparing to leave. Jordan had chosen to stay behind to prepare for the "investigation" that would take place later that night, when the two brothers and a single cameraman were locked in the house from dusk until dawn.

Now that his interview was over, Haven felt a bit silly for what he'd said. Then again, he had a feeling his agent and his publicist would love it.

"Do you believe it?" Pierce asked, as they bounced down the now-familiar dirt lane, heading back to the county road. "Do you really think she's still in that house?"

Haven shook his head and nudged his glasses back into place. "No. I don't believe in ghosts."

"But if she did haunt the house, you think she'd be benevolent?"

"I think she'd enjoy the hell out of trying to make you think otherwise."

Pierce chewed his lip thoughtfully as they turned onto the one-lane county road. Haven knew what Pierce wanted to ask him, but Haven wasn't ready to give an answer yet, so he hurried to ask a question of his own first. "What do you think? Do you really believe all this paranormal mumbo-jumbo?"

Pierce laughed. "I wish I had a dollar for every time somebody asked me that."

Haven felt chastised. The truth was, he could relate. People asked him all the time whether he believed the outlandish stories he wrote could be real.

"What you probably don't realize," Pierce went on, "is how much that night determined the course of our lives. I mean, it changed everything for Jordan and me. I know that sounds like something out of *Days of Our Lives*, but it's the truth. That séance? The whole thing with the well? It hit Jordan hard, not least of all because he knows how many people blame him for Elise's disappearance."

"So if he can prove that ghosts are real, it might help prove that he's innocent?"

Pierce nodded. "Exactly." They pulled to a stop where the county road met the state highway, and Haven waited while Pierce maneuvered them into traffic. They were drifting dangerously close to the question he knew Pierce would eventually ask, so Haven once again chose to drive the conversation in a different direction.

"What about you, though? What do you believe?"

"Like I said, that night changed both our lives. For Jordan, it was the séance. And you can sit there and act like it was all bullshit, but we both know something weird happened that night. Either Elise made the luckiest guess in history or that really was somebody else speaking through her."

He glanced toward Haven, as if weighing his reaction, but Haven wasn't sure what to say. As good as Elise had always been at pulling his leg, the séance *had* been above and beyond. "You said it changed both your lives. What about you? Was it the séance for you as well?"

"No. For me, it was that moment when you took the top off the flashlight and showed me why it wasn't turning on."

Haven blinked at him. "*That*? That's the thing that changed your life?"

Pierce threw him a wicked grin that made Haven's stomach feel like it was full of helium. "Not to belittle what happened between us later that night, but yeah, I guess it was. It was like you ripped back that curtain and showed me the man in the machine." He laughed. "Or the Elise in the machine, at any rate."

"And yet you still became a paranormal investigator."

"Yeah. Well…" He wrinkled his brow, thinking about it. "Our second year in college, Jordan became a bit obsessed with the paranormal. For me, it was only logical to go along with him and try to be the voice of reason."

"So your goal is to debunk it all?"

"Yes and no." They'd reached Haven's motel. Pierce pulled into a parking spot next to Haven's door, killed the engine, and turned toward Haven. "After everything we've seen, I no longer have the luxury of being a skeptic. Not completely, at any rate."

"So you've definitely seen ghosts? Is that what you're saying?"

"I don't know if they were ghosts or residual energy or something else entirely, but I've definitely seen things I can't explain."

Haven thought about Pierce's TV show. Sometimes it was eerie, no two ways about it. But sometimes, Pierce himself proved that what they were hearing was nothing more than squeaky floorboards or loose siding. But, of course, Haven had no way of knowing how much of what he saw on *Paranormal Hunters* was real and how much of it was staged by the producers to make it more dramatic.

It was almost as if Pierce knew what Haven was thinking. "I understand why people are skeptical. Some people in this line of work are too quick to blame every creak or cold draft on ghosts. In reality, I'd estimate we find logical, non-paranormal explanations for about eighty-five percent of what we find."

"And the other fifteen percent?"

Pierce grinned. "That's the fun part." He sobered quickly though, leaning closer to Haven in his eagerness to explain. "Remember when I told you earlier that Jordan and I do other investigations in our free time?"

"Of course."

"The places we're invited to investigate can generally be broken down into one of two categories. The first are private residences or small businesses—things like a small-town library or a pizza parlor—where people have encountered something they can't explain. And we're human, so our first reaction is fear. These people want us to come in and either tell them no, there are no ghosts, there's a logical explanation; or they want to hear that if there are spirits, they're not dangerous. And most of the time, they're not."

"Most of the time," Haven said. "But sometimes they are?"

"We've both come out of investigations with scratches or burns we can't explain. It's rare, but it happens."

"What happens then? Do you perform an exorcism or something?"

Pierce shook his head definitively. "Not our area. We have a list of people we can refer them to if they want something like that done."

"Okay. So what's the second type of location?"

"The second type are what you see on the show. Places like the Lizzie Borden house, or the Bell Witch Caves, or the Pennsylvania Penitentiary."

Haven nodded, seeing where Pierce was going with his story. "Places that rely on their reputation of being haunted for their business."

"You got it."

"Are the places like that as haunted as they claim?"

"Not in my experience. Which isn't to say they aren't haunted at all. Just that they aren't necessarily any *more* spiritually active than various private residences I've investigated over the years. It kind of goes back to our previous discussion about urban legends versus reality. Legends are big. They make people more receptive to suggestibility, but they're just that— legends. Not fact."

Haven had to admit he was intrigued. "Give me an example."

"Okay. The Stanley Hotel is a good one. Have you been there?"

"The place where Stephen King supposedly wrote *The Shining*? No."

"There are lots of claims that the activity there is amplified by high concentrations of quartz and magnetite in the soil. So, back in 2008, Bryan and Baxter—this paranormal investigation team in Colorado—decided to stop taking people's word for it and find out for sure. They started making calls, asking if any real tests had been done. They hadn't, but these various governmental agencies were intrigued by the idea of playing ghost hunter for a bit, so they all showed up at the Stanley and spent a few days digging in the dirt and running all kinds of tests. Want to guess what they turned up?"

"Nothing?"

"Exactly. They found soil, just like all the other soil in the area. The final report by the USDA was presented to the owners. But still, if you go up to the Stanley to take one of their ghost tours, I guarantee you'll hear all about their mythical magnetite and quartz."

"Why bother investigating if everybody's going to ignore it anyway?

"The thing is, just because there's no quartz at the Stanley doesn't mean there's no activity. I mean, I've been there. That place is damned creepy, quartz or not. The concert hall is freaky as hell. But places that rely on tourism don't necessarily want the truth. They like the legends. They survive off the legends."

"So the show mostly focuses on the second type, but in your free time, you go check out the others? The private homes? Places like that?"

"As much as we can, yeah. When you have a scared family just wanting to know their house is safe, it's a whole different ball game. They're way more open to what we have to say."

"Still." Haven shook his head. "It must be frustrating."

"Sometimes." Pierce's eyes were bright. He clearly enjoyed talking about his work, if nothing else. "That's not the hardest part though."

"What is?"

"I guess the thing that pisses me off the most is that nobody will call it science. It doesn't matter how many degrees Jordan and I have. It doesn't matter how careful the investigators are to explore every logical explanation. 'Real scientists'"— he made air quotes around the words—"still roll their eyes at us. And I get it. I mean, history is working against us. All the most famous mediums and spiritualists of the nineteenth century were revealed as frauds. Too many charlatans have used trickery and lies to make money over the years. And yet, over a hundred years later, we're still being condemned for what they did."

"You don't think that's fair?"

"Chemists in that same time period were still trying to turn lead into gold, but we haven't used that as an excuse to ignore the entire field of chemistry. The thing is, even if there aren't ghosts, that doesn't mean there isn't something going on. Maybe it isn't what we think, but we could still learn something by studying it."

"Wait. So they might not be ghosts, but it's still paranormal?"

"Maybe. Maybe not."

"You've lost me."

"Okay. Let me give you a non-paranormal example. Loch Ness."

"As in Nessie, the Loch Ness monster?" Haven asked, unable to keep the disbelief out of his voice.

"Aha! See, that's exactly what it comes down to. Did you know Loch Ness is actually a pretty unique lake? You can't see anything in it, because of the peat content. The water's practically black, which makes it easy to imagine all kinds of crazy stuff. Based on surface size, it's the second-largest loch in Britain, but based on volume of water, it's the biggest. It never freezes. It's deeper than the North Sea, and some people think there could be underground passages connecting them."

"Okay," Haven said, confused as to Pierce's point. "So what?"

"So, whether the Loch Ness monster is real or not has nothing to do with whether or not we still have things to learn. The fact of the matter is, Loch Ness is unique, and there are things there worth studying. But as soon as any biologist says the words 'Loch Ness,' they're laughed right out of their tenure, even if their study had anything to do with mythical monsters."

"I see." By this point, Haven was turned halfway in his seat as well, facing Pierce over the center console of the rental car. "So you accept that the things you've encountered in your investigations may not be paranormal, but—"

"But there are still things we can't explain! Look at our EVPs."

"The recordings you make on the little microphones, and claim to hear voices in?"

Pierce laughed easily, despite the jab. "Sure, ninety percent of the time, it's just white noise and our brains insist on looking for patterns that aren't there, but I've been there. I've been in a highly controlled environment, with no radio interference at all, and I've come out with a recording of a clear, distinct voice. Not just random words, either. I'm talking about full sentences."

"Like what?"

"One said, 'She left it by the river.'"

"Who left *what* by the river?"

Pierce gripped Haven's wrist, excitement written across his expressive face. "I have no idea, but who cares? It was a voice. Yet, it's immediately written off as a hoax. But it wasn't a hoax, Haven. I was there. I swear to God, it might not be a ghost, but it's *something*."

Haven found himself smiling, unwillingly infected by Pierce's enthusiasm, and the twinkle of intrigue in his eye.

Jesus, he was still gorgeous enough to take Haven's breath away.

"Tell me what you're thinking," Pierce said.

Haven felt himself blush. No, he wasn't about to admit his exact thoughts. "Nothing, really."

Pierce's smile faded a bit, becoming something more somber, and Haven knew he'd run out of time. Pierce was going to ask him the question he'd been dreading.

"Do you still think my brother did it?"

Haven sighed, focusing on the place where Pierce gripped his wrist. "I don't know."

"Lance's confession doesn't change anything for you?" There was no mistaking the anguish in his voice. "It doesn't at least make you question what you thought you knew?"

"I didn't say that."

"Haven..." He waited until Haven met his gaze. "You once asked me if my brother and I had some kind of psychic link."

"I remember." He remembered everything about that night. "You said you didn't."

"I told you the truth. But psychic link or not, I know my brother. I can tell when he's lying. He isn't lying about this. He's embarrassed about what happened that night. He's ashamed of the way he acted, but he didn't hurt her. I know he's telling the truth about that. And I *know*..." He leaned closer, his voice dropping to almost a whisper. "I know he's innocent."

Haven closed his eyes, struggling, although he wasn't sure why. For so many years, he'd blamed Jordan. He'd been so sure. Now, having heard Lance's confession, he had his doubts, and yet he was strangely reluctant to let his surety go.

But at the same time, he trusted Pierce. He always had.

"Haven?" Pierce prodded.

Maybe his certainty meant nothing at all. Maybe it was a crutch at this point, like blinders on a horse, preventing him from seeing the truth. But hanging onto his anger wouldn't get him any closer to the truth.

He took a deep breath and let it go. As he did, he let his hatred of Jordan go too. He let Pierce's determination wash away the last of his doubts.

When that was done, he once again opened his eyes and met Pierce's gaze. "I believe you."

It was as if the simple words transformed Pierce before Haven's eyes. His shoulders went down, his grip on Haven's wrist loosened. A broad, easy smile spread across his handsome face. "Thank you."

At that moment, Haven wished more than anything that Pierce would do what he'd done all those years ago, when he'd leaned across the gap between them to kiss him. The memory of the one night they'd spent together was fresh and strong in his mind. They hadn't actually had sex. Not even close. It'd only been a bit of kissing and heated exploration. They'd been young and unsure and inexperienced, and yet everything between them had felt natural and comfortable, as if it were meant to be.

How different might things have been if Elise hadn't disappeared? He and Pierce might have spent the last two weeks of their summer together, exploring their sexuality, letting whatever existed between them deepen instead of dealing with the fallout of a disaster. Maybe Haven would have gone to Ohio State instead of WVU. They might have been each other's first true love.

It was a lot to assume, all these years later, but it seemed so clear, like a beaten but promising path glimpsed through the woods.

One denied to them both, until now.

Haven's empty motel room was only a few steps away. He debated inviting Pierce in. They could start again right where they'd left off. A bit of innocence lost, maybe, but now they could come at it with more experience and a great deal more maturity on each side. Would Pierce welcome the chance to try again? Haven had no idea if Pierce was out with his family, or if he was even single. He also had no idea how much time they had before Pierce had to be back at the Gustafson house to start the investigation.

He opened his mouth, ready to find out, but at that moment, Pierce's phone buzzed.

Pierce let go of Haven's wrist, ending their moment of intimacy as he pulled his phone from his pocket to check the screen.

"Shit."

"Problem?" Haven asked, wondering if Pierce could hear the disappointment in his voice.

"Just Jordan and Jeremy having another one of their arguments. I'm always expected to be the peacemaker." He put the phone away and turned to Haven with an apologetic smile. "Thanks for what you did today."

Haven didn't want to ask what that meant—whether it was his spontaneous answer in the interview about Elise's ghost, or admitting that Jordan might not be a killer, or something else entirely. He was just glad to have Pierce's approval.

Twelve years had gone by, but it seemed he still hadn't managed to grow up.

CHAPTER 13

Twelve Years Ago

Haven dreamed of the purple worbles.

He was six or seven years old, running around with Linsey and Elise and some of the older neighborhood kids on a hot, sticky summer evening, long after the sun had gone down. In theory, they were playing Kick the Can, or maybe Ghost in the Graveyard, but in reality, Haven had no idea what he was supposed to be doing. All he knew was that it was dark, the streetlights transformed the familiar neighborhood of his childhood into a mysterious maze, and his mom hadn't yet called him inside.

It was one of those wild, magical moments that would forever epitomize the glorious freedom of his youth.

"Stay out of the shadows," Elise said, suddenly appearing at his side. She would only have been eight or nine at the time, but in his dream was nineteen and beautiful. "The purple worbles will get you."

"The purple what?" Haven asked, already wary of anything Elise told him.

"The purple worbles. They're ugly little men who live under the street. Once it's dark, they come up through the asphalt. But only in the shadows."

"What happens if they catch me?"

"They'll drag you through the storm drain, down to their lair. They'll lock you in a cage for a while, but eventually, they'll eat you."

"You're making that up."

"I'm not. They got Jim's dog last week."

"Did not!"

"Did so." Elise turned to call across the street, "Hey, Jim!"

Jim, who lived two houses down from Elise, turned their way. "What?"

"Tell Haven about your dog."

The streetlight above him clearly illuminated the confusion on his face. "My dog?"

"Yeah. You know. The one who got taken by the purple worbles."

"The wha—"

"Remember when the purple worbles dragged Scrappy down the storm drain?"

Boom, boom, boom!

Haven sat straight up in his sleeping bag, still chasing the thought of some dog he'd never even seen being dragged to its doom.

"What was that?" Pierce mumbled, without moving from his spot on the floor. The two of them had eventually fallen asleep, side-by-side, but each in their own sleeping bag.

"I don't know—" Haven started to say, when the sound came again.

Boom, boom, boom.

It was somebody pounding on the bedroom door.

"Haven, let me in!"

Haven wrestled free of his sleeping bag. "It's Linsey." He shivered as he padded in his sweats across the bare, wooden floor.

"Haven!" Linsey cried again.

"I'm coming!"

He'd barely unlocked the door before she burst in, her face streaked with tears. "Oh my God, Haven. I was so scared. I swear I heard somebody in the hall. I heard voices, but there's nobody else here—"

"Where's Craig?"

"He thought he heard Elise and Jordan arguing outside, and he was still so sure we should tell the police, so he went out there—"

"Wait. What? When?"

"He went out looking for them, but he's been gone for ages!"

"Did you check downstairs?"

She shook her head, sniffling, then wiped her nose on the back of her hand. "I can't go down there."

Haven looked over at Pierce, who was now wide awake and sitting up, his sleeping bag puddled around his hips.

"Will you go down and look for them?" Linsey asked, gripping Haven's arm. "Please!"

Haven sighed, but didn't debate for long. He needed to use the bathroom anyway. "Okay. Settle down. Just give me a minute to get dressed."

"I'll come with you," Pierce said, standing up.

"No, don't leave me alone!"

"Linsey," Haven said, gripping her arms. "You'll be fine. You have your flashlight, right?"

No. She didn't. In her panic, she'd left it in her room. Haven found his glasses, then went with her to retrieve it. The door to Elise and Jordan's room was wide open. A quick glance inside proved it was empty. Their sleeping bags lay spread out, side-by-side on the floor, but it didn't look like they'd been slept in. Haven glanced at his watch and was shocked to find it was just after three in the morning.

They definitely should have been back by now.

He got Linsey calmed down and settled in his room with her flashlight, then he and Pierce went quietly down the stairs.

"They probably fell asleep in the living room," Pierce said.

But nobody was in the living room. A quick search of the rest of the ground floor convinced them that Craig, Jordan, and Elise weren't in the house.

"Let's check outside."

They stopped first on the front porch to empty their bladders over the railing. The woods were forebodingly silent. Not a single sound reached their ears.

They took their flashlights into the backyard. Still, they heard nothing. Haven searched the trees for the flicker of flashlights, but found no sign of his friends. They called their names—quietly at first, then louder—but got no reply.

"Where could they have gone?" Haven asked.

"I don't know."

"You guys are twins. Don't you have some kind of psychic connection or something?"

Pierce laughed. "No, thank goodness. I don't want to know what he's doing with Elise. I'm pretty sure he doesn't want to know what I was doing with you earlier tonight either."

Haven ducked his head, his cheeks warming as he remembered.

"Listen," Pierce said, stepping closer and lowering his voice. "If anybody asks, I brought a deck of cards. We spent an hour or two playing Five Card Draw, then went to sleep. Sound good?"

"Were we playing for money?"

"No. Just for fun."

"Who won?"

Pierce laughed. "I'd say it came out about equal, wouldn't you?"

Still, despite his lighthearted tone, Haven knew he was worried about his brother. He noted the tension in Pierce's shoulders and jaw. "Maybe they went back to the car."

"For what?"

Haven shrugged. "For a bit of privacy, I guess." He shivered. "And to crank the heat."

"Maybe. But what about Craig?"

"I don't know." Haven pulled his jacket tighter around him. He wanted to be back in his bag, sleeping next to Pierce. Preferably with*out* Linsey in the room.

"Okay. Let's think about this rationally," Pierce said, "If one of them was hurt, the others would have come back and woken us up, right?"

"Probably."

"Even if they were lost, they'd be within shouting distance. We would have heard them, I think."

"Yeah, I think so too."

"And séances aside, what else could have happened to them? I mean, it wasn't a yeti. It wasn't little green men or the swamp thing."

"Maybe it was the purple worbles."

"What?"

"Nothing. Sorry."

"All right. So…maybe they went back to the car, like you said."

Even though Haven had been the one to suggest it, it sounded weak to his ears. But he didn't have any better suggestion to offer. "Maybe."

"Nothing could have happened to them. Not to all three of them. Which means wherever they are, they're together, and they're fine."

That seemed logical. "So what do you think we should do?"

Pierce shrugged. "Go back to bed and hope they're here by morning."

CHAPTER 14

Present Day

Haven spent the entire evening wishing he knew what was happening at the Gustafson house. Would Pierce and Jordan encounter anything? Would they hear Cassie speak or see Elise's ghost? Haven imagined every possible scenario—some boring, some absurd, and some utterly horrifying. He wished Pierce would at least text him, but he never did. Haven supposed they weren't allowed to use their cell phones while filming.

The investigation required that Pierce and Jordan be up all night, so Haven knew he wouldn't hear from Pierce until the following afternoon, at the earliest. Just after three o'clock, somebody knocked on his motel room door. Haven took a second to shove his dirty clothes out of sight before letting him in, glad he hadn't made too much of a mess in the couple of days he'd been there.

"How'd it go last night?" he asked, once Pierce was inside.

"Not so good." There were no bags under Pierce's eyes, and no other obvious signs of weariness, but he sounded tired nonetheless. "We came up with a whole lot of nothing. Not even a hit on the EMF meter."

"Oh." Haven tried to remember which one of the gadgets he'd seen on the show Pierce was referring to, but came up blank. "I'm sorry."

"Whatever." Rather than taking one of the two chairs in the room, Pierce threw himself backward onto Haven's bed to stare at the ceiling. "Listen. I have a question to ask you. Are you free tonight?"

"Of course. Why?" The possibilities intrigued him.

"Well…" Pierce rubbed his eyes with the thumb and finger of one hand. "I want you to know, this wasn't my idea. I'm just the messenger."

"Okay. What?"

Pierce sat up, leaning forward with his elbows on his knees. "Jeremy'd like you to join us tonight, for the second night of the investigation."

"At the house, you mean?"

A stupid question, in hindsight, but Pierce simply nodded. "Yeah. How do you feel about that?"

Haven sank into the armchair in the corner of the room. He'd seen enough episodes of *Paranormal Hunters* to be intrigued. There was also the simple fact that he still had his own questions about Elise's séance. If it really had been Cassie talking to them on that night, was there a chance she'd do it again? The possibility scared him, but hot on the heels of his fear came his memory of Elise, alive and smiling, utterly in her element in the Gustafson house.

Was it possible they could finally learn what had happened to her?

Pierce was still watching him, waiting for his answer. "Sure," Haven said at last. "Yeah, I'm in."

Pierce's smile was small, but grateful. He stood up. "Excellent. Let's go, then."

"Already?" It wouldn't be dark for a few hours.

"Yeah. That'll give me a chance to show you how it all works first."

"What about dinner?"

"I'll make sure you don't starve, trust me." He glanced at Haven's suitcase, propped in the corner. "Bring your jacket. It gets cold in there." He laughed, as if surprised at his own words. "I guess you know that as well as I do."

They made the drive in silence until turning off onto the narrow, barely discernible trail. Haven was more freaked out than he liked to admit at the idea of spending another night in the Gustafson house. "Do you really think having me there will make a difference?" he asked.

Pierce shrugged, his expression unreadable. "Maybe. If it's Elise we're dealing with."

Haven thought about his certainty from the day before. "She always did love scaring the crap out of me."

Pierce smiled, not taking his eyes off the road. "That's sort of what Jeremy's counting on."

The area around the Gustafson house had been transformed since Haven had last seen it. In addition to the second truck, an enormous, square tent had been erected in the middle of the overgrown front yard. The low hum of a generator filled the air. At least half a dozen men and women milled around between the tent and the house.

"Who are all these people?"

"The part of the show you never see," Pierce said, putting the car in park. "Come on. Let me show you around."

Inside the tent, the *Paranormal Hunters* crew had set up a command center of sorts. One wall held an enormous bank of monitors and a long plastic table covered with computer equipment. Some of the monitors showed the living room; others were blank. Based on the activity around them, Haven figured the crew was still setting up.

"We have cameras up in the house," Pierce said, confirming Haven's thoughts. "Some full spectrum, some infrared, some thermal imaging. Even a few old-fashioned trap cameras." He must have noticed Haven's confusion, because he explained. "It's a camera with a motion sensor. Hunters use them. It'll use an infrared flash to take photos if anything triggers it." He pointed again to the monitors. "Most of the cameras are in the living room, but we're setting some up around the staircase, as well. Everything comes back here, real-time, where the rest of the crew watches for anomalies. We have a few microphones planted around too." He pointed at a man sitting at the end of the table wearing heavy headphones. "Tony there will be listening to what we get off of those. Jordan carries a little digital recorder in his pocket too, although he only turns it on once in a while."

Next, Pierce led him to the other side of the tent, where a table was littered with small electronics. Haven had seen most of them used on the show before, but it still seemed a bit surreal to have Pierce put one of them in his hand.

"EMF meter," Pierce explained. "It measures magnetic fields, which tells us if a spirit is trying to draw power. In a house with no electricity, there shouldn't be much, but it's still good to have with us. This one over here's a digital thermometer, so we can detect cold spots or sudden drops in temperature." He pointed to one that was cylindrical, with several small light bulbs on the top. "You've probably seen this on the show. It's a REM pod. It detects magnetic fields too. Any changes in the field around the pod will cause the bulbs to light up." He held up something that looked like a hand-held radio. "This is the spirit box. It uses radio frequencies to allow spirits to talk to us."

His tone was odd, and Haven raised an eyebrow.

Pierce glanced around the tent, and shook his head. "I'll tell you later," he mumbled, setting the device aside.

He led Haven through the busily working people toward the house. A few of them turned to watch Haven pass, but no one said anything.

"A lot of people on our crew read your books," Pierce said, giving Haven the first genuine smile he'd seen from Pierce all afternoon. "They're probably wondering if it's okay to ask for your autograph."

"My autograph's overrated, believe me. It's Elise who should get all the credit."

He felt Pierce's weighted glance, but didn't turn to meet it. "Not all of it, I don't think."

Haven shrugged, uncomfortable, as he always was when people tried to praise him. He concentrated instead on not tripping as he climbed the house's rickety front steps.

Two other crew members labored in the living room of the house, but Haven didn't get a good enough look to see what they were doing. He and Pierce found Jordan in the kitchen, where a small buffet of deli meats and cold salads had been laid out on the countertops. He glanced up from the sandwich he was making.

"Wow. Pierce talked you into it after all. I didn't think you'd do it."

"Not like I had anything better to do tonight." Besides, Elise would have liked it. Haven almost smiled, thinking about it.

Pierce picked up a plate and began his own sandwich preparation. "Help yourself," he said over his shoulder to Haven.

Haven eyed the trays of meat, sliced cheese, and fruit. "Is this normal?"

"When local law enforcement tells us to keep a low profile, yeah. And after your little run-in with Chief Fuller the other day, this seemed like the safest bet." Jordan finished spreading mustard and put the halves of his sandwich together. "We'll clean it all up before we start filming, though."

They took their sandwiches and cans of pop onto the back porch. There was no railing—just a flat, elevated surface, approximately six-feet square, less than two feet off the ground. Jordan sat on the steps, Pierce sat with his back against the wall of the house, and Haven perched on the edge of the porch, his legs hanging over. The sun was low in the sky, its light filtering through the leaves, reminding Haven of the picture they'd shown him of the well. The sky was perfectly blue and, in the pure light of day, the woods around them seemed peaceful rather than menacing. They ate in silence, soaking in the last of the day's heat.

"It's actually pretty nice out here, isn't it?" Haven asked, after setting his empty paper plate aside. He had to turn sideways to be able to see both brothers from his place on the porch. "Funny how it isn't spooky at all during the day." But then he eyed the house. "Well, not *too* spooky, at any rate."

Pierce laughed, craning his neck to eye the house. "It's in better shape than you might think. The front porch needs to be rebuilt, and the whole thing needs a paint job, but the house itself is still sound."

"You can tell his degree's in structural engineering, can't you?" Jordan asked.

"One of my degrees," Pierce corrected. "Electrical engineering too."

"Show off."

Haven knew they'd both gone to college at Ohio State, but he'd never known what they majored in, or even if they'd graduated. "What about you?" He asked Jordan.

"Physics."

"Wow." That was surprising, given his current occupation. "I majored in literature. Sort of a waste, I suppose, but it made sense at the time." It was strange, sitting here with them after so many years. Especially after his certainty that Jordan had killed Elise. "Listen, Jordan—"

Jordan held up a hand to stop Haven's apology. "Forget it. It was a logical conclusion to jump to. Especially before we knew about Elise's affair with Mr. Gustafson."

Still, what had been comfortable suddenly felt awkward. Haven studied his empty pop can, searching for some casual way of changing the subject. Luckily, Jordan saved him by turning to Pierce and saying, "Did you tell him?"

Pierce's cheeks flushed. He suddenly seemed unwilling to meet Haven's eyes. "No."

"Tell me what?"

The brothers eyed each other for a second, having one of their strange, silent debates. It was Jordan who finally broke the silence.

"We tend to disagree with Jeremy about certain things. He likes us to always have the lights off in the house during an investigation, because it makes it spookier. We prefer to mimic the conditions in which actual encounters happen. He likes to use all the fancy equipment people send him. We prefer to stick to more basic tools. What we tend to do is compromise. Last night, we had all the lights off, the way he likes it. But we stuck to simple cameras and REM pods for the investigation, the way Pierce and I like to do it."

"We came up empty," Pierce said. "A big, fat zero."

"Which is bad for ratings." Jordan's tone was difficult to interpret. "Especially since they're hoping to make this into a two-part episode to kick off the next season. So, tonight, we're changing things up—"

"While still compromising," Pierce added.

"Right. Which means we're using more of Jeremy's equipment than we like."

"Like the spirit box?" Haven asked.

Both brothers nodded, but it was Pierce who answered. "It shuffles through radio frequencies and emits white noise. The theory is that spirits can use them to communicate."

"The thing is," Jordan picked up the tale, "we've always sort of believed it'd be a lot easier for a spirit to just knock, or trip the REM pod, than for them to manipulate radio frequencies."

"Plus, the spirit box is noisy as hell," Pierce added.

"So you don't think it works?" Haven asked.

Pierce shrugged, but let his brother answer. "Some people have great results using it, but it's never been our favorite tool."

"We'll be using one tonight, though?"

Jordan nodded. "We promised Jeremy we would. But see, the other side of the compromise is that we do things our way as far as the setting is concerned."

"Meaning what?" Haven asked.

"Meaning, we try to mimic the conditions of previous encounters."

Haven turned to Pierce, his heart suddenly pounding. "Is he saying what I think he's saying?"

Pierce at least had the good graces to look ashamed of himself. "Yeah. I'm afraid so."

Haven gulped, remembering. "We're going to hold a séance?"

Jordan looked way more excited than Haven felt. "Exactly."

Haven spent the next couple of hours signing autographs and answering questions for crew members while the brothers went over logistics with Jeremy and Todd. Haven had assumed Jeremy would be inside with them during the investigation, but Pierce explained that he'd monitor from the production tent instead.

Once it was dark, they began filming. They started by making a big production of locking Pierce, Jordan, and Haven inside the house with Todd, the cameraman, which was a bit absurd since the house of course locked from the inside. They could always just undo the deadbolt, open the door, and walk out, if they really needed to. But nobody pointed that out.

Jordan spent a while using his handheld digital recorder in different parts of the house, asking questions, then playing the recording back, listening for answers. He came up blank each time. Pierce seemed unfazed by the lack of response, but Haven could tell it frustrated Jordan.

"Forget it," Jordan finally said. "Let's do the séance."

Todd turned off the camera while the brothers prepared. They had a box full of candles, which Jordan began setting in a circle, just as Elise had done. Pierce took Haven's hand and pulled him down the hallway, to the office with the card tables where they'd talked the first day. Haven was pretty sure he'd chosen that room because there were no cameras set up there. Pierce closed the door behind them, then set his flashlight on end on the tabletop, giving them a small bit of illumination in the otherwise pitch-dark room.

Still, his face was mostly in shadow when he turned to face Haven. "I feel like an ass for not telling you about the séance before you agreed to come tonight."

Haven shrugged. "I don't think it would have changed my mind."

"So you're okay with this?"

"I think so." Although now that it was almost time to begin, he was more nervous than he liked to admit. Was it possible his cousin was nearby? Was there really a chance he'd get to speak to her? "Do you think it will work?"

"I have no idea." Pierce moved a bit closer. "First we'll try it the way we did when we were kids. But if we don't get something pretty quick, Jeremy's adamant that we use the spirit box."

"Why? Does he think it's more effective?"

Pierce shrugged uncomfortably, but took a moment to consider his answer before responding. "The thing is, humans tend to be receptive to suggestion."

"You're saying we're gullible."

"That's not the word I'd use. But we tend to find things we're told to look for."

"What do you mean?"

Pierce scrubbed one hand through his hair, thinking. "Okay. Let's say I stand in front of a room full of people with a little vial of water. I tell them it's peppermint oil. Then I open the vial and spill it on the floor. I tell them to raise their hands the minute the smell of peppermint reaches them. Without fail, about half the people in the room will eventually raise their hands. Now, are they lying? Or is just the thought of peppermint oil enough to convince their brain they smell it? And if their brain *thinks* they smell it, and our brains create our reality, then how is thinking we smell something any different from *actually* smelling it?"

Haven shook his head. "I have no idea."

"Well, neither do I. But it works with things like this too. I've seen it done in mock séances. A group of people will decide who they want to talk to, and every single time, at least one of them will swear they hear that name come through the spirit box. But did they actually hear it, or was it all in their heads?"

"So you want me to be skeptical?"

"Absolutely. But I want you to be open-minded too."

"Skeptical, but open. Got it."

"Haven." Pierce's voice was quiet. He moved closer again, this time taking Haven's hand. "Listen—"

"Pierce!" Jordan's yell from the living room interrupted. "Where the hell are you? Stop flirting with Haven and get out here so we can get this over with."

Well, that answered the question of whether or not Pierce was out with his brother. Pierce dropped Haven's hand and turned away. Haven wondered if Pierce was actually blushing. "We're coming," he called toward the hallway. Then, quieter to Haven, "You ready?"

Haven was still nervous, but his fear was moderated by a bit of excitement as well. "I think I am."

Jordan was waiting for them in the hallway. He eyed them suspiciously as they exited the room. "Maybe you forgot we're supposed to be working?" he said to his brother, his voice a low growl.

"Maybe you forgot it's none of your damned business."

Haven wished he could disappear rather than watch them argue, especially since the argument seemed to be over him. It was the first time he'd ever seen them be genuinely short with each other. The cameraman looked as uncomfortable as Haven felt.

Haven stepped into the living room and forgot all about his discomfort. The candles had been set up in a circle, just as they had been that night, twelve years earlier. Three small votives sat in the middle. Haven's heart burst into high gear.

"You ready?" Jordan asked from behind him. Haven wondered if he was imagining the bit of anger in his voice.

"Yes."

"Good. Todd, why don't you film from that corner over there, by the fireplace? That'll give you a good view of the circle and of the stairs, just in case something happens on the landing."

"Sure thing."

Todd did as instructed. Haven, Pierce, and Jordan settled on the living room floor. The REM pod sat between them, along with a bottle of absinthe, and the three lit votives.

Haven gulped, his mouth suddenly dry. Only a minute earlier, he'd been ready for anything. He'd been skeptical and excited. Now, all he felt was anxiety and sadness.

Would he ever stop missing his cousin?

"Our circle's quite a bit smaller than it was last time," Pierce said, his tone assuring Haven he knew how he felt.

Haven could only nod his agreement.

"Are you ready?" Pierce asked.

How many times were they going to ask him that? Haven nodded again, before realizing Pierce was talking to Todd, the cameraman.

"We're rolling," Todd said.

"Okay." Jordan's tone was all business now. Whatever anger he'd felt toward Pierce and Haven was either gone or well hidden. He seemed calm and confident as he addressed the camera. "We're here in the Gustafson house. We're about to recreate the séance we had twelve years ago, when the ghost of Cassie Kennedy spoke to us."

Haven wanted to argue. They didn't know whether or not Cassie had really talked to them. For all they knew, it had just been Elise pulling their leg. But it was Jordan and Pierce's TV show, not his, so he kept his mouth shut.

Jordan brought the bottle of absinthe forward. He did as Elise had done, pouring a bit into the cap and setting it in the center of the circle. He then handed the bottle to Haven.

"Take a drink."

Haven glanced toward the cameraman. "I thought you couldn't show people drinking on TV."

"Total myth," Pierce said. "We're only drinking a little, to recreate what happened twelve years ago. We won't drink enough to get stupid."

When they'd first done this, Haven had barely wet his lips. This time, he took a healthy pull off the bottle. It wouldn't have been his first choice of alcohol, but if it would help steady his nerves, he'd take it. He handed the bottle to Pierce, who took a drink before handing it to Jordan. They passed it around a second time, and then Jordan set the bottle behind him, out of the way.

"You guys ready?"

Pierce nodded. Haven couldn't even manage that, but Jordan didn't wait for an answer.

"Let's hold hands like we did that night."

Pierce was on Haven's right, just as he had been twelve years earlier. But now, instead of Linsey's ice-cold fingers on his left, he had Jordan.

"Good," Jordan said. "Now, we're going to repeat the same thing we did back then. I'll start, and you guys join in." He turned his attention to the candles in the center of their circle. "Spirits of the past, come to the light. Move among us on this night. Spirits of the past, come to the light. Move among us on this night."

Haven's nerves were temporarily overcome by embarrassment. It sounded as silly now as it had when he was seventeen.

As if reading his mind, Pierce smiled over at him, quickly squeezing Haven's fingers, before joining his brother. "Spirits of the past, come to the light. Move among us on this night. Spirits of the past, come to the light..."

Haven took a deep breath and jumped in. He felt like a moron, but his publicist would love it. "Move among us on this night. Spirits of the past, come to the light. Move among us on this night."

They droned on, their voices finding an easy, shared rhythm. The absinthe in Haven's stomach warmed him. He rarely drank hard alcohol, and he thought it was already making his brain a bit fuzzy.

"Spirits of the past, come to the light. Move among us on this night. Spirits of the past—"

The candles flickered, and the lights on the REM pod suddenly flared to life. Their chant died. The hair on Haven's arms and the back of his neck stood on end. His palms felt hot and sweaty. He desperately wanted to break their circle so he could wipe them on his jeans.

"Is somebody here with us?" Jordan asked. "Cassie, is that you? Do you remember us from twelve years ago?"

The lights on the REM pod blinked off, but the air still felt oddly charged. Haven's skin tingled.

"Who's here?" Jordan asked. "Is it Joseph? Or maybe..." He glanced at Haven, his eyes almost apologetic. "Elise? Is that you?"

Nothing.

"Can you trip the REM pod again?" Jordan asked. "Just touch it, and the lights will turn on. Let us know you're here."

The lights on the REM pod flickered, so quickly on and off again that Haven wasn't entirely sure he'd seen it at all.

"One more time," Jordan said. "Try to keep the bulb lit so we know it's you."

Nothing happened with the REM pod, but Todd broke the silence to say quietly, "The EMF readings are all over the place. There's definitely something here."

Jordan nodded without looking Todd's way. "Are you still there?" he asked. "We have something else here that might help you communicate with us." He let go of Haven's hand long enough to pull the spirit box from behind him. "I'm going to turn this on, and you can use it to talk to us, if you like."

He flicked a switch. A harsh, loud noise, somewhere between a hiss and a buzz, assaulted Haven's ears, like an old-fashioned radio set on an empty frequency, with the volume turned to the max. It was like the rumble of a chainsaw reverberating in the back of Haven's skull. It ran for a few seconds at a time, with a strange little hiccup of silence in between, creating a *zzzzz, zzzzz, zzzzz* pattern that Haven thought might drive him crazy if it went on too long. Jordan placed the box in the center of their circle, along with the candles and the REM pod, and took Haven's hand again. Haven realized too late he hadn't used the break to dry his damp hands. He could only hope the twins weren't too grossed out.

Zzzzz, zzzzz, zzzzz, the box went, like a loud swarm of bees, setting Haven's teeth on edge.

"Are you here?" Jordan called. He had to raise his voice to be heard over the box's incessant buzzing. "We'll start again, and you can use the box to talk to us any time you like." He glanced around at Haven and Pierce. "Ready?"

This time, Haven managed to nod.

They began anew.

"Spirits of the past, come to the light. Move among us on this night. Spirits of the past, come to the light. Move among us on this night." They chanted louder this time, their pace somehow quickened by the frantic *zzzzz, zzzzz, zzzzz* of the spirit box. Haven's backside was beginning to hurt. It made him feel old. It'd taken a lot longer than this to make him uncomfortable when he was seventeen, that was for sure. "Spirits of the past, come to the light. Move among us on this night. Spirits of the past, come to the light. Move among us on this night."

His skull ached too, pounding in time with the spirit box's whine. No wonder Pierce hated to use it.

"Spirits of the past, come to the light. Move among us on this night. Spirits of the past, come to the light. Move among us on this night."

And suddenly the box's noise changed.

Zzzzz, zzzzz, zzzzz—aven—*zt.*

They stopped chanting, both brothers staring directly at Haven. The box went on with its *Zzzzz, zzzzz, zzzzz.*

Haven swallowed, wondering if he'd heard correctly. Wondering if it was all in his head. Pierce had warned him that people often heard whatever they'd been told to expect. Was that all that was happening now? Was it only his imagination?

"Cassie?" Jordan called. "Is that you? Or is this Elise?"

*Zzzzt, zzzzt, zzzzt—*AVEN—*zt.*

It reminded Haven of the walkie-talkies his family had used on their lake trips when he was a kid. There was a trick to it. If you pressed the "talk" button and started speaking too soon, the person on the other end wouldn't hear the first few letters of whatever you had to say. Likewise, if you let the button go as soon as you finished speaking, the person on the other end wouldn't catch the last few letters either. You had to depress the talk button, wait a second, then speak. When you were done, you had to wait another second, then release. But his dad never got the hang of it. Everything he said through the walkie-talkie came out strangely abbreviated. Instead of "Come down to the boat," Haven would hear "—m down to the b—."

The spirit box seemed to have a similar issue. Still, Haven felt certain he'd heard his name. Judging by the stares Jordan and Pierce were giving him, they'd heard it too.

Zzzzt, zzzzt, zzzzt, zzzzt, zzzzt—

"She wants you," Jordan said, just loud enough for Haven to hear him over the buzz. "Talk to her."

Haven swallowed, trying to figure out what to say.

Zzzzt, zzzzt, zzzzt, zzzzt, zzzzt—

"Elise?" he said, his heart pounding so hard he could feel it all the way to his toes. "Is that you?"

*Zzzzt, zzzzt, zzzzt—*AVEN—*zt.*

But after their last séance, Haven was skeptical. "How do I know it's you?" he asked. "How do I know this isn't Cassie or Joseph?"

*Zzzzt, zzzzt, zzzzt, zzzzt, zzzzt, zzzz—*orbl—*zzt.*

Haven felt the blood drain from his face. Pierce and Jordan's expressions were predictably confused, but Haven knew what she'd said.

Worbles.

Purple worbles.

Haven opened his mouth, wanting to say something, but nothing came out. This was his cousin. He was sure of it. This was Elise, who'd been missing for twelve long years. Tears pricked at the backs of his eyes. He had the sudden urge to put his face in his hands and cry. "It's her," he said, his voice cracking. "It's Elise."

"Elise," Jordan said. "I know it's hard for you to talk to us like this. I know it takes a lot of energy. But we really need to know where you are?"

Zzzzt, zzzzt, zzzzt, zzzzt, zzzzt—

They waited, listening.

Zzzzt, zzzzt, zzzzt, zzz—ELL—zzt, zzzzt—

Haven's heart skipped a beat. The shock on Pierce and Jordan's faces mirrored his own feeling.

Did she say what he thought she'd said?

"Elise," he said, his voice shaking. Just saying her name brought tears to his eyes. "Elise. Who killed you?"

Zzzzt, zzzzt, zzzzt, zzz—ent—zzt, zzzzt—

Click.

The spirit box died. The sudden silence after its constant racket left Haven's ears ringing. A gust of icy air from his left raised the hair on the back of his neck and extinguished every candle in the room, plunging them into darkness.

The front door remained shut tight, the windows boarded up. Haven could find no easy explanation for the sudden breeze or the goosebumps on his arms. The two brothers still held Haven's hands, both of them squeezing so tight, his fingers ached.

"Is she gone?" Jordan asked, his voice barely a whisper.

"Elise?" Haven asked, his stomach tight. He wanted to wipe the tears from his cheeks, but didn't dare let go of Jordan or Pierce's hands. He felt as if he couldn't get a good lungful of oxygen. The darkness was heavy and oppressive, but the strange charge he'd felt in the air had disappeared. He knew instinctively Elise was no longer with them.

"Shit," Todd said.

Haven jumped. He'd honestly forgotten the cameraman was even in the room. A bright beam of light stabbed through the darkness as Todd clicked his flashlight to life. Both brothers let go of Haven's hands at the same time.

"What happened?" Jordan asked.

"The camera's dead," Todd told him. "The battery's drained."

"The one in the spirit box too, apparently," Pierce said, inspecting the small device.

Jordan tried his flashlight but nothing happened. "She got mine too. Let me check the digital recorder."

Jordan, Pierce, and Todd jumped into motion, talking into their radios to the crew in the command tent, clicking on the lights set up around the room. They'd all shifted into work mode, and Haven felt abandoned.

"What happened?" he asked, his heart still pounding. His hands shook as he dried his cheeks.

"Paranormal activity often drains batteries," Pierce said without looking up from what he was doing. "Just give us a minute."

No, Haven wanted to say. *What happened during that séance? Did you hear what I heard?* But the words stopped in his throat.

What *had* he heard anyway? Had Elise really spoken to him?

Two crew members came through the supposedly locked front door, bringing a new camera and, presumably, new batteries for the other equipment. The room now felt crowded, the strange eeriness completely gone. Everyone seemed to have forgotten Haven, including Pierce, so he turned and walked quietly out of the room, up the stairs, into the bedroom that Elise had never gotten around to sharing with Jordan.

He wanted to go outside but he wasn't sure if that was allowed. He needed to breathe. He still felt as if the air in the house couldn't provide the oxygen his brain needed. He expected the window to be stuck shut after so many years of disuse. Luckily, it took only a bit of effort to slide it open. He put his forehead against the screen and gulped in the cool, night air, letting it dry the last of the tears from his cheeks.

Outside, everything seemed peaceful, despite the crew moving about on the lawn. The monitors inside the production tent caused it to glow in the darkness. I wasn't enough to drown out the stars overheard though. An owl hooted somewhere off to the right. It should have been comforting, but Haven felt as if his entire world had been shaken to its very foundation.

He'd talked to Elise. After twelve years of wondering, he'd spoken to his cousin.

"Are you all right?"

He'd hoped for Pierce. He got Jordan instead, followed by Todd, his camera on his shoulder, although Haven knew he wasn't filming because the lens pointed at the floor. Haven wasn't sure he was ready to face him anybody yet, but he did it nonetheless, turning away from the open window. "I think so."

"I know this is unnerving, but it's best if we go over it now, while it's still fresh. Are you okay with that?"

"Unnerving" didn't begin to cover how Haven felt, but he took a deep breath and nodded. "Sure. Let's do it."

"Good." Jordan glanced at Todd, who hefted the camera into position and gave Jordan a thumbs up. Jordan turned back to Haven, his demeanor shifting from friendly to all-business. "Okay, Haven. Now that we have fresh batteries and we've had a few minutes to think about what happened, I'd like to ask you a few questions."

Haven nodded, because that felt like the right response. He wasn't used to going through everything twice, repeating everything a second time for the camera. "All right."

"We definitely received a response during our séance. Would you agree?"

A shiver ran up Haven's spine. "Absolutely."

"Tell us what you heard."

"What do you mean? You were there! You heard it too, didn't you? Or…" Suddenly, he doubted himself more than ever. "Was it just me? Did I imagine it all?" After all, it was nothing but white noise. Any odd hiccup could have sounded like a word, if that was what he'd wanted to hear. Haven was dismayed to realize he was close to tears again. "Jesus, did my brain just make it all up? Was it nothing but delusions?"

"Don't," Jordan said, his voice gentle. He sounded just like Pierce would have. "Don't do that to yourself. You know what you heard. You know what you felt."

"Do I? Because the more I think about it, the crazier it sounds! It's just like Pierce said—I expected to hear something, so I did. That doesn't make it real."

"It doesn't make it fake, either," Jordan said.

"But—" Haven didn't know where this protest was going. He threw up his hands. "Jesus, you're not helping at all." Jordan and Todd glanced at each other, both of them looking as if they were trying hard not to laugh. Haven's frayed nerves snapped. "What's so funny?"

"Nothing." Todd made an obvious effort to stifle his amusement, but couldn't quite quell his smile.

"It's just that this is how it goes," Jordan said. "Welcome to the world of paranormal investigation. Even when you experience something first hand, you're left with more questions than answers and no proof whatsoever."

Haven's anger fell away. He had a newfound sympathy for the brothers. "I never thought of it that way."

"You have to walk that fine line between skepticism and openness," Jordan said. "You don't want to immediately accept everything as paranormal, but you also don't want to dismiss your instincts as irrational. Know what I mean? On some level, I think you *know* what you heard. But only you can decide what to do with it. Is it easier to tell yourself that you're losing your mind than to accept that somebody spoke to us tonight?"

Haven shook his head. "I don't know."

"Okay. That's fair. Let's just go one step at a time. The first thing she said was your name, right?"

Haven nodded. "Yes."

"How many times did you hear your name?"

"Three times."

Jordan nodded. "That's what we heard too. But then you asked her to prove she was Elise, and she said something I didn't understand. Something like 'orbles' or 'warp holes'?"

Haven blinked in surprise. It seemed he wasn't completely crazy. Jordan had heard it too, even if he hadn't known what it meant. "Worbles. The purple worbles. It was a story she told me once when we were kids, to scare me. The worbles were these little men she claimed lived under the street. They'd come up out of the shadows and drag people into the sewers."

"And then what?"

"Eat them." Haven smiled at the memory.

Jordan furrowed his brow. "That sounds a bit like that book you wrote."

Haven nodded. "It is. All of my stories come from her. Sometimes I feel like a fraud for writing them at all."

He knew instinctively that Pierce would have objected to that statement, but Jordan had other things on his mind. "So she did what you asked and confirmed it was her. It had to be Elise who spoke to us."

"I guess." But that still seemed like too much to admit at once. He wasn't quite ready to accept he'd conversed with a ghost.

"What about the rest? All I caught of the next word was an 'L' sound at the end."

"That's what I heard too. My first thought was 'hell,' like she's in hell, but then I figured she said 'well,' but…" He shook his head. "I might be assuming too much."

"You're right to be skeptical. It'd be easy for us to jump to that conclusion because of what happened here when we were kids, but she could just as easily have said 'will' or 'still' or 'call' or... anything."

Haven could only nod.

"And then the last word. What did you hear?"

"'Ent.' Except it isn't even a word. I have no idea what it means. What did you hear?"

"I thought she said 'sent.' Does that mean anything to you? I mean, anything that specifically relates to Elise, the way the worbles did?"

Haven shook his head. "No."

"Pierce heard 'ant.' I assume that doesn't mean anything to you?"

"No." Haven shook his head. "Ant. Ant. Wait. What if it was 'aunt,' like a relative?"

"Would that mean anything, though? Is it possible one of her aunts killed her?"

Haven thought about it, but the obvious answer was no. The only aunt in the region had been his own mother, and he was quite sure she hadn't been involved. He felt utterly defeated. "No. I'm sorry. I have no idea what she was trying to tell us"

Jordan waited, as if hoping Haven would go on, but what else was there to say?

"Okay," Jordan said to Todd. "Let's cut there for the moment."

Todd nodded and lowered the camera. Haven turned to look out the window again as the cameraman left the room. The production tent still glowed faintly from within, but all the foot traffic between it and house had ceased. It seemed they were ready to get back to the investigation. "What happens now?" he asked Jordan.

"We'll try to reach her again, but my gut tells me we'll fail. She used up everything she could to tell you that much. I think the rest of the night will be dead."

Haven sighed and leaned his forehead against the screen. For just a moment, he'd felt close to his cousin again. The idea that she'd slipped back out of reach bothered him more than he might have expected. "So our big breakthrough was to hear her say 'ant'?"

"Don't lose hope," Jordan said.

Hope. It was something he'd given up on years ago. Just hearing the word made Haven's eyes suddenly sting and his throat tight. "Why did we come back here?" he asked quietly.

"You came back for answers," Jordan said.

"And you?"

"I came because it was what my brother wanted."

That surprised Haven enough that he turned to look at Jordan. He'd thought it was the other way around—that Pierce had come to help clear Jordan's name. "I thought he came here for you."

Jordan shook his head. "That may be what he told you. Hell, it may even be what he told himself, but it's a lie. He came for the same reason he did twelve years ago." His gaze was intense enough to make Haven blush. "For you."

Haven gulped, his mouth suddenly dry. "What do you mean?"

Jordan scowled in exasperation. "Come on, Haven. You know exactly what I mean. Are you trying to tell me you can't see it in his eyes every time he looks at you?"

Haven's limbs suddenly felt lighter than air, like his hands and legs might float away, leaving his pounding heart and his too-slow head behind. He resisted the urge to grin. It seemed like the wrong time and place for it, after what had happened during the séance. But the knowledge that Pierce might still be interested in him after all these years made him practically giddy. "I…uh. Wow. I had no idea."

"Well now you know." Jordan lowered his voice, taking a step closer. "Just do me a favor, all right? Cut him loose. Twelve years of carrying a torch for you is enough. If you care about him at all—"

"Jordan!" Pierce's voice reached them from the ground floor. "Haven? Are you guys done up there or what?"

"We're coming!" Jordan called back, before turning back to Haven. "If you care about him at all, you'll let him move on."

Haven wearily followed Jordan back down the stairs, feeling intrigued and chastised. Jordan's obvious disapproval bothered him. If it'd been disapproval simply because Haven was male, he might have blown it off as narrow-mindedness. But this seemed to be more personal. Jordan didn't think Haven was good enough for his brother.

The problem was, Haven secretly agreed with him.

Still, the idea that Pierce had been "carrying a torch" for him all these years certainly piqued his curiosity.

Pierce's gaze flicked between them as they entered the room, the tiny wrinkle between his eyes when he looked at Jordan hinting at his annoyance. "Is there a problem?" he asked, the question clearly directed at his brother.

"No problem here," Jordan said with a smile. "We're ready to try this again. Todd, help me get the candles lit."

Pierce raised an eyebrow at Haven, begging the question. Haven shook his head. "I'm fine."

He didn't think Pierce believed him. It was true he was tired and overwhelmed. He would have loved a minute alone with Pierce, but he wasn't going to get that anytime soon, so there was no point dwelling on it.

They settled again in a circle on the floor and went through it all again. And again.

And again.

The endless repetition of Elise's stupid phrase made the syllables turn to jumbled mush on Haven's tongue. He still muttered them in unison with the twins, but the words ceased to have any real meaning. He was especially caught up on "among."

A-mung.

A. Mung.

Was that even a word? Who the hell had come up with this stupid chant anyway?

"Forget it," Jordan said at last. "She's gone."

Haven groaned as he got to his feet, his knees popping as if he were forty years older than he really was. His backside had gone numb. His brain felt like overcooked oatmeal.

"What time is it?"

"Just after two," Pierce told him.

Lord, he'd never felt so tired. How could just sitting there on the floor wear him out so much?

"We have a couple of hours left," Jordan said. "I think we should try to get some EVPs up by the banister, where Joseph hung himself."

Pierce glanced at Haven. "You look dead on your feet."

"Oh, good. That's about how I feel, so at least I'm consistent."

"We can finish up without you, if you want to curl up somewhere for a nap."

It seemed like a good plan, although it didn't take Haven long to realize there wasn't any place comfortable. He didn't think he was allowed to open the front door and go to the car. He didn't want to interrupt Pierce and Jordan's work to ask. In the end, he chose the office on the ground floor. It'd at least been swept clean. It still held two rickety card tables and a few folding chairs. Haven sank down on one of the latter with a sigh of relief. At least it was the type of folding chair with a bit of cushion built into the seat. He took off his glasses, laid his head on his arms on the tabletop, and managed to fall right to sleep.

He dreamed of chasing Elise through the trees.

It was soft and unfocused. Unlike other dreams he'd had of her in the past, it didn't feel frantic or urgent. He wasn't desperate to catch her. He felt exhilarated, running down the moonlit path, staying out of reach of the purple worbles. He couldn't quite see Elise, but he knew she was there, just ahead of him and around the bend, waiting to jump out and scare the crap out of him simply because she could.

Her laughter echoed all around him.

"Haven," Pierce whispered an indeterminable amount of time later, gently shaking Haven's shoulder. "Wake up. Time to go home."

Haven sat up and rubbed his eyes. He was stupidly thankful he hadn't drooled all over the table in his sleep. "What time is it?"

"Just after four."

"You're done?"

"Yeah, we're done. Let me drive you home. Or, you know...back to your motel, at any rate."

Haven followed him outside, slowly coming more awake in the cool morning air. The sun wasn't quite rising, but the gentle brightness of the sky hinted at dawn and reminded Haven of his dream.

The production tent hadn't come down yet. Some of the crew stumbled around, looking as tired as Haven had felt before his little nap.

"We're lucky," Pierce told him as they climbed into the car. The dome light showed Haven the dark circles under Pierce's eyes before he closed the door. "When we do investigations at places with business hours the next day, we have to clean up everything before we go home. But we have permission to be on the property through tomorrow, so most of the crew will come back in a few hours and finish loading up."

"Did you get anything else?" Haven asked as Pierce turned the car around and pointed it toward town. "Any EVPs?"

Pierce shook his head. "Not a darn thing."

"I'm sorry."

"Don't be. That séance was pure TV gold. Jeremy was practically foaming at the mouth." He glanced Haven's way briefly before turning back to the road. "How do you feel about what happened?"

"Talking to Elise, you mean?"

Pierce's weary expression gave way to a hesitant smile. "You willing to believe that's what it was?"

Haven considered the purple worbles. "I can't think of any other explanation."

"How's it feel to no longer have the luxury of being a skeptic?"

"I'll let you know when I'm a bit more awake."

They rode the rest of the way in silence. Pierce pulled into a parking spot outside Haven's motel, and Haven turned to face him, ready to say goodnight.

Come on, Haven. You know exactly what I mean. Are you trying to tell me you can't see it in his eyes every time he looks at you?

In that moment, Haven saw what Jordan meant. Now that he knew what to look for, it was as clear to him as the five o'clock shadow on Pierce's face. What Haven had taken for cautious friendliness in Pierce was more like a silent plea. It had been Haven who'd ended their relationship years ago, not Pierce. He'd wondered if Pierce would welcome a chance to try again. Now, he knew the truth—Pierce had only been waiting for Haven to give him a sign.

Haven had been afraid before, but not now. "You want to come in?"

A slow smile spread across Pierce's face. "I've always wanted to come in."

Haven's stomach buzzed with excitement as he led Pierce inside and closed the door behind them.

First things first, though.

Pierce used the restroom, then ceded the space to Haven. Haven spent a bit longer than he intended freshening up—washing his face and brushing his teeth. When he finally emerged, he found Pierce splayed across the bed on his back, sound asleep.

Haven chuckled to himself. He debated waking him, but the truth was, he was exhausted as well.

There was always tomorrow. Pierce wasn't going anywhere. Haven had no doubt at all he'd still be around in the morning.

Haven undressed and eased under the covers, doing his best not to disturb his bedmate, even though Pierce was taking his half of the bed out of the middle.

Haven didn't mind one bit.

CHAPTER 15

Twelve Years Ago

Haven woke with a crick in his neck from sleeping without a pillow. Weak sunlight filtered through the dirty windows, making the room brighter than it had been at any point since their arrival the night before. A glance at his watch told him it was 6:30.

Had any of their friends returned after he'd fallen back asleep? If so, he hadn't heard them. Linsey and Pierce were still sleeping. Every rustle of fabric and creak of the floorboards seemed extra loud as Haven wiggled free of his sleeping bag, stretched the stiffness out of his limbs, and donned his shirt, jacket, and glasses. He tiptoed out of the room in his stocking feet and peeked around the corner into the other bedrooms.

No sign of Elise, Jordan, or Craig.

A dark sense of dread hung heavy in Haven's chest. Something about this was definitely very wrong. He hoped he'd find his friends in the living room, but he knew before he crept into the room they weren't there. The house was just too still. Even sleeping, their presence would have added a bit of sound and warmth. But the ground floor of the house was as empty and uninviting as before.

Where in the world had they gone? Had they wandered too far from the house and gotten lost? Part of him wanted to let Pierce and Linsey sleep, but doubt gnawed at him. Something was wrong. He knew it, on some instinctual level.

He was glad, upon returning to the upstairs bedroom, to find Pierce already awake.

"Anything?" Pierce asked quietly, the minute Haven stepped into the room.

Haven shook his head.

"Do you think they got lost?" Pierce asked, still whispering, so as not to wake Linsey.

The fact that they'd both had the same thought seemed to confirm it. It was the most logical answer.

Unless they'd gone to the car.

Haven pulled on his sneakers as Pierce got dressed. They descended the stairs, side-by-side, weighing their options as they went. They could walk back to where they'd left the vehicles. It was entirely possible they'd find their friends waiting for them there. But then they'd have to turn around and come back to the Gustafson house to collect their things. It seemed logical to pack up now and take everything with them to the cars. Except they had camping gear for six people, with only three of them to carry it.

And what if the others weren't in the cars? What then?

They spent a few minutes calling for their friends from the back porch, hoping against hope the lost trio were trying to find their way out of the woods now that it was light. The only thing they succeeded in doing was waking Linsey, which meant starting the entire debate all over again, this time with Linsey's input.

Their options hadn't improved.

"Okay," Pierce said, after they'd gone in circles over it for another fifteen minutes. "They're either lost or asleep in the cars. The only way to know for sure is to go see. We don't want to make two trips, but I don't see that we have an option. The three of us can't do it in one trip, no matter what. So I vote we take as much as we can. Then, when we find those assholes cuddled up in the back seat, we make them come back for the second load."

It was as good a plan as any.

They left the house half an hour later, their arms loaded with sleeping bags and duffels. They called for their friends as they made their way through the woods, but the only sounds they heard were birdsong and the chatter of irritated squirrels.

"This is just like Jordan," Pierce griped as they walked. "He's always coming up with harebrained schemes, then leaving me to clean up after him."

He seemed annoyed, although less worried now that they had a plan. Haven's doubt nagged at him more than ever. He glanced over at Linsey. She was clearly fighting back tears.

"It's just like Craig too," she said quietly. But it was what she didn't say that scared Haven the most.

Leaving them to clean up the mess they'd made was *not* like Elise. Not at all. She liked to prank people, but she wasn't selfish. She was always the first to jump up and help their mothers clean up after Thanksgiving or Christmas dinner. She volunteered to babysit their younger cousins. She let Linsey borrow her clothes, makeup, and jewelry without even asking. She'd even let Haven borrow her car on multiple occasions. Yes, she'd taken them to the Gustafson house in hopes of scaring the hell out of them, but disappearing afterward was completely out of character.

Haven tried to tell himself she'd be at the car. He tried to convince himself that there was no reason to worry.

He didn't succeed.

But the three of them continued to call into the trees. "Elise! Jordan! Where are you? Can you hear us?"

They were almost back to the cars when one of their calls received an answer.

"Stop shouting! You'll wake the neighbors!" It was Jordan's voice, and a few seconds later, as they rounded a curve, they spotted him coming up the road, looking mildly sheepish. "I planned on getting back to the house before you guys woke up," he explained, taking some of Linsey's load. "I guess I slept late."

"What happened?" Haven asked. "You decided to sleep in the cars?"

Jordan fell in step next to them. "Not exactly. It was more that the idea of walking back to that house all alone in the middle of the night didn't seem all that appealing."

Linsey and Haven stopped dead in their tracks.

"Alone?" Linsey asked. "Aren't Craig and Elise with you?"

Jordan shook his head without breaking stride. Linsey and Haven hurried to catch up. "Elise and I— God, it's just so stupid. She got this sudden urge for barbecue-flavored Corn Nuts. So we went back to the car and drove into town but then... Well, I guess we had a bit of an argument."

"About what?" Linsey asked.

"Just about the whole thing. Coming to the house. Whether or not it was haunted." It sounded innocent enough, but Jordan's cheeks were red. He seemed unwilling to meet anybody's eyes. "Anyway," Jordan went on, "she had me drop her off in town. She said she had a friend who would drive her home. She told me she'd be back here with her car first thing in the morning to help pack up."

"And what about Craig?" Haven asked.

Jordan shrugged. "I don't know. I never saw him. His car was here when Elise and I left, but gone by the time I got back."

They finally reached the cars—or *car*, singular, now that Craig's was gone—and loaded their gear. Haven's stomach grumbled. He wished he'd thought to grab a bite to eat before they'd started out. They'd left all their snacks back at the house. It suddenly seemed like a ridiculous oversight.

Still no sign of Elise.

They walked back to the house in silence. Pierce had obviously relaxed now that he'd found his brother. Haven knew he should have been relieved too, knowing Elise and Craig weren't lost somewhere in the woods, but the persistent feeling that something more was going on refused to wane.

They wolfed down some granola bars and pop for breakfast, cleaned up as much of the mess as they could—they were able to chip the dried wax off the floor, but the oily stain it had left behind would have to stay—and finally headed back to the car with the last of their stuff. There was no way to fit the four of them plus all their supplies into a single car. They idled about for a while, waiting for Elise, but when eleven o'clock rolled around with no sign of her, they gave it up for a lost cause. Jordan and Pierce hid their cooler in a copse of trees, saying they'd come back for it later. They crammed everything else into the trunk or the back seat, then piled inside. Jordan backed the car out of their parking spot and headed for town.

Haven glanced over at Linsey across the pile of sleeping bags between them. She tried to smile, but it didn't quite take. "I'm going to kill Craig," she whispered. "I can't believe he just left me like that."

"What about Elise?"

She shook her head, her eyes searching the forest, as if she might find Elise among the trees. "I'm not sure if I'm worried, or just really, really pissed."

"I know what you mean. I guess we'll decide once we find out where she is."

They dropped Haven off first. Pierce helped unload his bags from the trunk. Haven knew it was only so they'd have a moment of semi-privacy. He turned to Haven with the trunk still open, blocking them from Jordan and Linsey's view.

"Listen, I know you're worried, but Elise is probably at home, sleeping off a hangover."

"Probably," Haven agreed, although he didn't think it would be the case.

Pierce nodded, his eyes locked on the ground. He took a small step toward Haven, bringing them within inches of each other. "I, uh, well…" He cleared his throat. His cheeks were red, but he finally met Haven's gaze. "I just, well, I'm glad…"

He didn't seem to know how to finish that sentence, but it didn't matter. Haven knew what he meant. "Me too."

Pierce gave him a shy smile. ┆ wouldn't kiss him—not here, on the ┆ Haven's house, where anybody might se┆ Pierce gave him told him that he wished he co┆ settled for giving Haven's hand a quick squeeze.

"I'll call you later, okay? Maybe we can go to a ┆ something."

Haven's heart did a funny little flop. He knew he ┆ smiling like a fool. "That'd be good."

A minute later, Jordan, Linsey, and Pierce were gone, ┆ and so was Haven's moment of levity. Elise wasn't at home nursing a hangover, because she hadn't been drinking.

Unless she started at her friend's house, after Jordan dropped her off in town. It seemed unlikely, but it wasn't impossible.

Haven dragged his bags inside and tossed them in his room. He was on his way to the shower when the call he'd been dreading came.

"She's not here," Linsey said, the strain of unshed tears in her voice. "Her car is here, but she isn't. I don't think she ever came home at all."

Haven knew Pierce
'treet in front of
—but the look
4. Instead, he
THE WELL
1ovie or
vas

Present Day

Haven slept deeply for several hours. He surfaced eventually, drifting peacefully in that soft, hazy place, halfway between dreaming and wakefulness. Pierce's body was pressed tight against his back, his arm wrapped around Haven in a way that was warm and comfortable. Haven had no idea when Pierce had stripped down to his boxers and climbed under the covers with him, but he sure didn't mind. He nestled closer, relishing the lazy sense of arousal caused by nothing more than shared body heat and the gentle pressure of Pierce's morning erection against his backside. Part of him wanted to turn around and let things progress in the usual way, but the other part of him was perfectly content to lie there for as long as he could, enjoying the simple intimacy of the moment.

Eventually, Pierce stirred, his arm tightening around Haven's waist. He sighed, a long, soft sound of contentment that warmed Haven's heart.

"God, Haven," he mumbled, his lips brushing the nape of Haven's neck. "All these years. I can't tell you how many times I wished I was waking up next to you again."

Haven smiled, happier in that moment than he'd been in years. It felt as if nearly every wrong in his life had suddenly been made right. He'd always known he'd seen Pierce again, but he'd rarely even dared hope for anything as perfect as this.

Pierce splayed his hand across Haven's stomach, his fingers brushing the waistband of Haven's briefs, making his breath catch in his throat.

But Pierce's next confession surprised him.

"I'm sorry."

"For what? Being in my bed?"

Pierce chuckled. "No. I'm definitely not apologizing for that."

"Then what?"

"About the way things ended between us."

Haven closed his eyes, not wanting to think about that last day they'd had together. "It doesn't matter."

"It did matter, though, didn't it?"

"We were young—"

"Don't you wonder how different it might have been?"

Of course he did. He'd thought about it often over the years, but he also knew it could never have worked. Not when he'd been so sure of Jordan's guilt.

"Haven?" Pierce whispered, his hand drifting down Haven's hip.

Haven turned, still caught in Pierce's embrace, but wanting to see his face. "I don't want to talk about that."

Pierce smiled, pulling Haven tighter against him. "What do you want to talk about?"

"Nothing at all."

Pierce made a sound that was part laugh, part anguished moan. "God, I love the way you think."

He started at Haven's throat and worked his way down, kissing and caressing, until he'd pulled Haven's briefs out of the way and enthusiastically put his mouth to work there. Jesus, it felt good. Haven tangled his fingers in Pierce's thick hair and lost himself in it, not bothering to worry yet about reciprocation, or what their time in bed together would mean later. Pierce was hot and driven, yet tender in his attentions, and Haven rode the wave, blissfully adrift, until the urge to finish was almost more than he could bear. Then he used his hand in Pierce's hair to pull him back, not wanting things to be over quite yet. Pierce came up the length of Haven's body, his kisses more urgent now, as he worked to shed his boxers without breaking contact.

"Condoms," Haven whispered. "You have to let me up. They're somewhere in my suitcase."

"All the way on the other side of the room?" Pierce's throaty chuckle sent a wonderful tingle down Haven's spine. "That was really poor planning on your part."

"I know."

Pierce sat up, straddling Haven's hips. "Lucky for us, I was a bit more on the ball than you." He slid open the drawer of the bedside table to pull out a strip of familiar foil squares.

Haven laughed. "When did you put those there?"

"Last night, while you were in the bathroom." Pierce ripped one off, tossing the rest back in the drawer. "Didn't really mean to fall asleep before you got back."

Haven laughed again. He was glad they'd waited. They never would have had the energy or the stamina to last this long after being awake all night. And now, looking up at Pierce, he couldn't quite believe his luck. Pierce was perfect—trim and fit and stunningly beautiful. Haven felt ridiculously skinny and pale next to him. "This is crazy."

Pierce froze with the condom package halfway open, looking down at him. "What is?"

"You, being in my bed. You're so far out of my league."

"Since when?"

"Always, I think. You just never realized it."

"No way."

"I never understood how you could have picked me. You were gorgeous and popular, and I always had my nose in a book."

"Maybe I liked being the person who could make you look up from that book."

Haven thought about that. It sounded good, but it didn't quite add up. Pierce must have read the disbelief on his face, because he sighed—half in exasperation, half in amused defeat. "Fine. You want to know why I like you? Why I've *always* liked you?"

"Yes."

"Because you're fearless." He said it as if it were the most obvious thing in the world.

"What? Me? No I'm not!"

"You are. You always have been. In school, nothing ever fazed you. Even with all the work Elise went through to scare us twelve years ago, you were the only one who didn't fall for it."

"That was only because I knew her too well."

"How about last night, during the séance? Most people would have been scared when they heard their name come out of the spirit box. You barely even blinked."

"That's not true. I was—"

"Then, you invited me in like it was the most obvious thing in the world."

"Maybe, I guess, but—"

Pierce leaned closer, so they were face-to-face. "But the most important time was that night, in the bedroom. God, I'd been trying to work up my nerve for weeks, but I never would have been brave enough to make the first move. Then you just up and asked me to kiss you." He smiled, his eyes glowing with an admiration that Haven knew he didn't deserve. "See what I mean? Absolutely fearless."

Haven could hardly believe what he was hearing. "I wasn't fearless, though. I was scared to death!"

"But you did it anyway." He put his hand against Haven's cheek. "That's why I liked you. That's why I'm still crazy you about, after all these years."

"But... Jesus, that's nuts."

Pierce laughed. "For what it's worth, my brother would probably agree with you." He held the condom in one hand, then slid the other down Haven's stomach, drawing his attention back to the matter at hand. "I've answered your questions. Now you have to answer mine."

Given what Pierce was *doing* with that hand, Haven found it hard to focus on words. He didn't manage much more than a moan. "Yes?"

"Top or bottom?"

Haven's heart skipped a beat. They'd never gotten anywhere near this far in their one fumbling night together, and Haven was struck by the irrational fear that he'd say the wrong thing and Pierce would change his mind. Then again Pierce wouldn't have asked if he wasn't flexible, and twelve years later, Haven had enough experience to know exactly what he wanted.

"Top," he finally said.

"God, I was hoping you'd say that."

But that sure didn't mean Pierce ceded control to him. Far from it. Haven managed to do little more than hang on, clutching at Pierce, gasping as they moved together. Pierce was gentle yet strong; sure of himself and his own desires, but careful to meet Haven's needs too. In the end, they were both left breathless and spent, lying sated and happily exhausted in each other's arms.

"Jesus, Haven," Pierce mumbled, sounding like he was already half asleep again.

"I know," Haven answered quietly.

They'd waited twelve long years. It'd been worth it.

They didn't sleep long the second time. Haven rose less than an hour later. He left Pierce sleeping while he took a quick shower. He halfway hoped Pierce would wake up and decide to join him, but he didn't. Instead Pierce waited until Haven was finished before taking his turn in the bathroom. Haven was dressed by the time Pierce finally emerged, wearing nothing but a towel wrapped around his waist. His wet hair beaded his broad shoulders with water.

He looked damned good, and Haven felt suddenly awkward, given what had happened between them. He did his best to act nonchalant. "Tell me about Craig," he said.

Pierce stopped short halfway between the bathroom and the bed, his brow wrinkling. "What do you mean?"

Haven had used the time Pierce was in the shower to made two cups of coffee using the little in-room coffee maker. He concentrated on emptying a packet of powdered creamer into his cup so he didn't have to meet Pierce's gaze. "When you called me about meeting you here, you said Jordan blamed Joseph, and I blamed Jordan, but you blamed Craig." He stirred the coffee with the little plastic straw. "I had no idea you thought Craig was responsible. I'm just wondering why."

"I guess because it never made sense to me, the way he left Linsey partway through the night and never came back." Pierce apparently took his coffee black. He picked up the second cup, took a tentative sip, and grimaced. "Jesus, that's bad. Does that powdered shit help?"

Haven laughed. "Not really." He set his still mostly full cup aside. "Linsey said Craig heard Jordan and Elise arguing, and went out to find them."

"That's the thing though. I've gone over this with Jordan a thousand times, believe me. He says they never argued until they were in town. He doesn't think Craig could have heard them."

"But we know Craig didn't do anything to Elise at the house, because she left with Jordan."

"True, but Jordan said Craig's car was there when he and Elise left, but gone by the time he got back. It's always seemed a bit too neat and tidy to me, especially given the way his dad seemed to keep him separate during the investigation, like he was protecting him."

"So you think Craig followed them?"

"I do."

"Then what? He took Elise after Jordan dropped her off? And his dad was covering for him because he knew?"

Pierce swallowed the rest of his coffee in one gulp and tossed the empty paper cup into the trash. "I think it's a possibility."

"But why would he hurt Elise?"

"I don't know. Maybe he liked her more than we realized. Or maybe..." He shrugged. "Maybe he took her simply because he *could*. Maybe he saw an opportunity and he just couldn't pass it up."

"But he's a cop."

"He is *now*. He wasn't then. But frankly, it fits. Guys with power issues often gravitate to law enforcement."

Pierce dropped his towel and began hunting around on the floor for his clothes. The sight was unnervingly distracting, and Haven had to force himself to stay on track. "Have you talked to him since you got back in town?" he asked, as Pierce stepped into his boxers.

"No. Why?"

Haven tried not to stare too hard at the tempting line of hair trailing downward from Pierce's navel. "Maybe it's time we found out what he has to say?"

"Maybe." Pierce picked up his jeans, but didn't move to put them on. He eyed Haven up and down, a wickedly sexy glint in his eye. "You in any kind of hurry?"

"To talk to Craig? I guess not. He lives here in Hobbsburg. Not like he's going anywhere."

"Anything else you need to do today? Any meetings scheduled? Phone calls to make? Any pressing errands?"

"Well, I'd kill for some chipped beef gravy right now, and a decent cup of coffee. But other than that? No, I've got nothing. Why?"

A slow smile spread across Pierce's face. He dropped his jeans and pulled Haven close, bending to brush his lips up Haven's neck. "What do you say we order room service, then spend the rest of the afternoon in bed?"

Haven sure wasn't going to argue with that.

CHAPTER 17

Twelve Years Ago

A flurry of phone calls consumed the first few hours after arriving home. Elise's parents were predictably frantic, calling all of her friends' houses, trying to figure out where she spent the night. In between they called Haven's parents, Craig's dad, and the Hunter family. As the day rolled on, the entire story spilled out—how they'd gone to the Gustafson house to spend the night, then gone looking for a well in the dark. There were questions of how they'd gained access to the house. Haven's parents kept using the phrase "broke in," and it didn't matter how many times Haven told them they'd done no such thing. Of course, it didn't help that he didn't know exactly how Elise had gotten them through the door...

The only bright side to the whole thing was that their trespassing seemed to be the least of anybody's concerns.

When Elise still wasn't home by dinner, her parents called the police.

An hour later Haven found himself sitting between his parents on the living room couch. Craig's father, Sergeant Clarence Fuller, scowled at him from the armchair on the other side of the coffee table.

Haven went over it all from the beginning. He didn't care at this point about who might get in trouble for what. All that mattered was finding Elise. He admitted everything, from the stolen absinthe to finding Jordan the next morning. The only detail he omitted was exactly how he and Pierce had spent their time alone in the bedroom. If there was a chance it would have helped find Elise, he wouldn't have hesitated to admit the truth about that too. As things stood, though, he couldn't see how it mattered to the investigation at hand. He was glad Pierce had thought to give them a cover story.

Sergeant Fuller listened, but the truth was, he didn't seem all that concerned. No matter how much Haven stressed that this wasn't like Elise at all, Fuller seemed convinced that there was no need for alarm.

"The girl's nineteen," he said to Haven's parents before he left. "Probably just out sowin' her oats. Pushing the boundaries. Kids do this kind of thing. I'm sure she'll turn up in a day or two."

Haven didn't bother to point out that the euphemism of "sowin' oats" seemed far more applicable to boys than to girls, and most certainly didn't sound like his cousin.

The big question was, where had she gone after Jordan dropped her off? She'd told Jordan she had a friend who would take her home. After canvassing the houses in the area, the only friend who turned up was Judy Roberts, but Judy insisted she'd been in bed early that night and hadn't seen or heard from Elise at all.

Which meant either they were missing something or Jordan was lying.

Jordan managed to clear up one question for the police. He'd been on the front porch with Elise when she opened the door, and he insisted she'd had a key to the property. There was no way to confirm though, because Elise's keys couldn't be found. Presumably, she'd had them with her when Jordan dropped her off. Haven learned through his parents, who heard it from Elise's parents, that Sergeant Fuller had talked to the owner of the house, Lance Gustafson, who said he'd lost the key and had no idea how Elise had ended up with it.

Another dead end.

Twenty-four hours dragged by, each second ticking away like some kind of horrible countdown. Haven's sense of dread grew heavier in his chest until it felt like he was dragging around a lead weight. His aunt and uncle were frantic. His own parents kept looking at him askance, somehow both relieved, and yet afraid of him, as if he'd emerged unscathed from the burning wreckage of a fiery, brutal accident.

Haven began to understand their haunting looks when he overheard them talking one night.

"What if one of them did it?" his mother whispered. "It could have been an accident. Maybe they argued. Maybe one of them pushed her and she fell. She might have hit her head on a rock, and they tried to cover it up—"

His father had interrupted her at that point, his voice a harsh, angry whisper. Nothing else had been said, but the next morning, his parents, his aunt and uncle, and Sergeant Fuller went to the Gustafson house. Haven saw their grim expressions as they left. It was clear they were anticipating stumbling over Elise's body in the tall grass surrounding the house.

They returned at dusk with a mixed sense of relief and aggravation. They'd found no sign of Elise.

They printed fliers the next morning and stapled them to light poles from one end of town to the other. Haven went downtown himself and stood on the corner outside the video rental shop handing them out. Hobbsburg was a small enough town that at least a third of the people he encountered knew Elise in one way or another, but nobody had any useful information to give.

There were nearly a dozen small towns within an hour's drive of Hobbsburg. Several sightings of Elise were reported, but none of them panned out. Sergeant Fuller seemed convinced Elise had simply run away and was intentionally hiding, which caused a new flurry of rumors to go scuttling through the break rooms and taverns of Hobbsburg—maybe Elise had been abused at home. Maybe there was some dark secret she didn't want exposed, and starting a new life for herself had seemed like the best option.

Haven didn't believe that for a minute.

On Thursday, when Elise had been missing for five full days, Chief of Police Lawrence Daavettila insisted that all five kids involved be brought to the station. Parents were told to wait in the lobby, while Haven, Linsey, and their friends were put in a single interview room, all of them sitting in a circle in hard plastic chairs.

All of them but one, at any rate.

Haven wasn't the only one to notice. "Where's Craig?" Pierce asked.

Chief Daavettila was in his sixties and bald, with a bushy mustache that was at least twenty years out of date. He rubbed the back of his neck, looking uncomfortable. "He won't be here."

"Why not?" Haven asked.

"Because—"

"Because his dad's your sergeant," Haven said, sounding braver than he felt. "I guess the cop's kid gets a free pass, huh?"

Chief Daavettila frowned and held up a hand to stop Haven's words. "That isn't true at all. I've spoken with Craig at length. His father and I agreed there was no need for him to be here."

Jordan scowled. Pierce gave Haven a look he couldn't interpret. Haven glanced over at Linsey. Her eyes were red and swollen. She refused to make eye contact.

"Okay." Chief Daavettila rubbed his weathered hands together and leaned into the circle. They'd somehow ended up sitting in the exact same order they'd been in for the séance. The only difference was Craig's absence, and the fact that Chief Daavettila had taken Elise's place as their ringleader. "Up until now, Sergeant Fuller's been handling this case. We all expected Elise to turn up in a day or two, but at this point, it's pretty clear there's something more going on here."

"Took you long enough," Linsey muttered.

The chief of police ignored her. "I know you've all talked to Sergeant Fuller individually, but I thought it was time I quit chasing your parents around by phone and got you all here in one place so I could hear the story with my own ears. So…let's talk about what happened last Saturday night."

They went through it again from the beginning, telling the story in turns, haltingly at first, but gaining momentum as they went. Haven and Jordan did most of the talking. Jordan dwelled on the séance, although it was clear Daavettila had no interest in that part of the story. Pierce and Linsey mostly stayed silent, simply nodding as Haven and Jordan told the story.

Right up until they reached the part of the tale surrounding the hunt for the well.

"Now here's where things get interesting," the Chief said. "Because up until this point, all of you had been together. But suddenly, you decided to split up. Why was that?"

"Because we were tired," Haven said. "It was cold and dark and late, and we were never going to find the darn thing. The rest of us were sick of Elise's game."

The Chief nodded, as if he'd known this part already. He turned his piercing stare on Jordan. "All except for you. You kept looking."

Jordan squirmed a bit in his seat, now that the focus was entirely on him. "For a bit, yeah."

"Then what?"

Jordan squirmed a bit more. "What do you mean?"

"What I mean is, you were apparently the last one to see her. Whether you like to admit it or not, she stayed outside, alone with you, and then she was never seen again."

Jordan's face flushed. Pierce scowled. Linsey and Haven exchanged a questioning glance. Could Jordan have done something to Elise?

"I didn't hurt her," Jordan said. "I didn't do anything. I've told you already—"

"You told Sergeant Fuller," Daavettila said. "Now I'm asking you to tell me."

Jordan sighed, but nodded. "Fine. Yeah. I stayed outside with her, looking for the well."

"But you didn't find it."

"Right."

"Then what happened?"

Jordan picked at a cuticle, staring at his hands as he talked. "Elise said we should go for a drive. I told her she was crazy, but she said no, it'd be fun. She kept talking about how she was dying for some Corn Nuts and a slushy. I said it was freezing, why in the world would she want a slushy, and then she said how the car would be warm and..." He stumbled, his cheeks turning red. "And romantic."

Haven shifted uncomfortably in his seat, resisting the urge to glance at Pierce.

"So you went back to the car?" Chief Daavettila prodded.

"Yeah. And we went into town and got her stupid slushy."

The Chief nodded. "We've confirmed with the clerk on duty that you were both there, and that Elise was fine when the two of you left. So where'd you go after that?"

"Elise suggested we park by that playground on 7th Street, so I did. We sat there for a bit while she finished her slushy, but then she said it was too far to drive all the way back to the house. She said she was tired, so we should each just go home for the night, then drive back out and meet our friends in the morning. I said that was stupid because everybody would wonder what happened to us. She said fine, forget it, I could do whatever I wanted, but she wasn't going back to that house to sleep. I said I'd drive her home. She said she didn't need a ride, that she had a friend on that street who'd take her."

He sighed, sounding frustrated. "It pissed me off. I'm sorry, but it did. I'd only agreed to the whole stupid idea because of her. Because we were supposed to, you know, to be together. And so…" His cheeks turned a deeper shade of red. He kept his eyes on his fingers. His fingernails had been chewed so close to the quick, they'd bled and scabbed over in some places. He looked miserable. Haven almost felt sorry for him. "I tried to kiss her." He glanced around at them all, looking defensive. "I mean, that was why we all went out there to begin with, right?"

Nobody answered. They all sat staring back at him with a mixed sense of horror and dread.

"What happened next?" Daavettila asked, his voice gentle.

"She sort of tried to pull away. I thought she was just playing hard to get, so I kissed her harder. And she shoved me away, really hard, and she slapped me." He put his fingers to his cheek, as if he could still feel the sting.

"That must have made you pretty angry."

Jordan scowled. "I said, 'I thought you liked me,' and she…" He glanced around again, obviously wishing he didn't have to say all this in front of his friends. He slouched lower in his seat. "She laughed at me. She said I was just a kid, that she was only trying to be nice. And so, I— well—" He opened and closed his mouth a few times, but he seemed to have run out of things to say.

Because he didn't know how to explain what had happened next?

"Did you hit her back?" Chief Daavettila finally asked. "Did you get so mad that you struck her?"

Jordan pulled back, appalled. "No! No, I'd never hit a girl. I just… Well, I called her a tease, all right? Because that's what she was. I mean, she knew I'd only gone out to that stupid house because she said she'd share a room with me. She unrolled her sleeping bag right next to mine. She practically promised we'd be together. Then suddenly she's slapping me for trying to kiss her?"

"Did you push her?" Daavettila asked. "Did you struggle, or have a fight? Maybe you wanted to make her to give you what she'd promised."

"No!" Jordan blinked at him, as if he couldn't believe what he was hearing. "No. Like I said, I called her a tease. I said, 'Why did you agree to share a room with me if you don't even like me?' And she said, 'I never thought we'd be there that long.'"

He stopped. For several seconds, the only sound was the *tick, tick, tick* of the clock on the wall. Chief Daavettila scooted closer to Jordan, his chair legs scraping discordantly against the concrete floor. "What do you think she meant by that?"

Jordan shrugged, hanging his head. "I have no idea."

The room fell silent again. Haven cleared his throat and forced himself to speak. "I do." They all looked at him, as if surprised to find he was still there. "She took us out there to scare us," he explained. "She figured we'd be too chicken to spend the night there. She probably figured by the time her séance was over, we'd all be jumping at shadows, begging to go home."

Chief Daavettila's expression was impossible to read. "I see." He leaned back in his chair and crossed his arms, turning back to Jordan. "Go on, son. What happened after she told you she never planned to spend the night with you? Did you get mad? Maybe you were just trying to get her to make good on her promise, and things got out of hand."

"I called her a bitch." Jordan sounded predictably dejected and embarrassed. "That's all. I told her to get the hell out of my car." He looked down at his hands, which were clenched together between his knees. "So she did."

"What happened next?" Daavettila asked.

Jordan shrugged halfheartedly. "I drove away."

"You weren't worried about how she'd get home?"

"Right at that moment? No. But then after I'd gone a few blocks, I felt bad, so I turned around. I figured the least I could do was drive her home, but by the time I got back to 7th Street, she was gone."

"You're saying she just disappeared into thin air?" The Chief was clearly skeptical.

"She told me she had a friend on that street who would take her home. I just figured she'd gone to her friend's house."

"But we talked to Judy Roberts. She says she never saw Elise that night."

He threw up his hands. "I don't know where she went, all right? I only know what she told me. She wasn't where I'd left her, and I didn't see her anywhere. I even drove up to her house, just in case she was walking. I figured I'd see her on the way. I thought I could pick her up and apologize, but I never found her. And so... I went back out to the Gustafson house. Or at least, I want as far as where we'd parked the car, and I slept in the back seat until morning. I never saw Elise again."

Haven wasn't sure if he believed Jordan or not. Either Jordan was lying and he'd killed Elise and dumped her body somewhere, or he was telling the truth, in which case, somebody else had seen Elise after Jordan. Somebody had picked her up, maybe even offered her a ride home. Whoever that person was...

Haven just hoped they'd be found.

CHAPTER 18

Present Day

They didn't spend the entire afternoon in bed. They eventually rose and went in search of Craig Fuller.

Craig had never married. He lived in a doublewide trailer on the eastern edge of town. He didn't exactly look pleased when he found Pierce and Haven on his front step, but he didn't look surprised either. He opened the door wide enough to allow them inside.

"I had a feeling you'd show up eventually." He wore his uniform shirt, but based on the way it was untucked and unbuttoned, leaving a plain white undershirt visible, Haven suspected he'd recently finished his shift. Craig glanced out the door, toward the car. "Jordan isn't with you?"

"We're meeting up with him later," Pierce said.

Haven didn't think he was imagining the look of relief on Craig's face.

"Have a seat."

The inside of his trailer was tidy, but it wasn't enough to hide the threadbare couch or the sagging chairs. The only thing in the place that looked less than ten years old was the flat-screen TV, where the Braves were playing the Cardinals. Craig left the TV on, but used the remote to mute the sound.

"You guys want a beer or something?" he asked as Haven and Pierce settled on the couch.

They declined, but Craig didn't let that stop him. He opened a bottle of Corona before taking the seat across from them.

"So, how's it going out there?" he asked, sounding genuinely curious.

"At the Gustafson house, you mean?" Pierce asked.

"Where else?" He shook his head, his eyes losing focus as he thought back. "Sometimes I think I want to go back out there. Sometimes I think, she must be there, you know? It's the only explanation. But it's private property, and to tell you the truth, the place still scares the piss out of me." He chuckled a bit, but suddenly sobered, his eyes going a bit wide. "You're not recording this or anything, are you?"

Pierce laughed, shaking his head. "Why does everybody think I have a camera hidden up my sleeve?"

"Well, I was thinking more of those little recording things you guys use. But I'll tell you, it's hard enough getting the kids in this town to respect anybody in a uniform. I don't need something like that reaching their ears."

"They won't hear it from us," Pierce assured him.

"Good." Craig contemplated the beer bottle in his hand. "That was the main reason my dad was so dead-set against me appearing on the show. I would have done it, but…"

When it became clear he wasn't going to finish that sentence, Pierce said, "It's fine."

"Well." Craig's gaze lifted reluctantly to meet Haven's. "I don't figure you came all the way here just to catch up."

Pierce and Haven exchanged a glance. They hadn't really come up with any kind of plan, but Haven figured there was no need to beat around the bush. "We want to know what happened to you that night."

"My story hasn't changed, if that's what you're wondering. I was telling the truth."

"The thing is," Pierce said, "none of us ever got to hear your side at all. Your dad kept you out of it, while the rest of us took the heat. You can't blame us for being curious."

Craig's jaw clenched. "I took plenty of heat from my old man, for what it's worth." He sighed, relenting. "But I suppose I see your point."

"What do you think happened to Elise?" Haven asked.

Craig shifted uncomfortably in his seat, his eyes drifting to Pierce, then quickly away.

Pierce obviously noticed too. "You think my brother did it." It was more a statement than a question.

"It's the only thing that makes sense."

Pierce scowled, and Haven hurried to head off the argument before it began.

"Tell us what happened to you that night. You told Linsey you heard Jordan and Elise arguing, but Jordan doesn't think that's possible. So what made you leave Linsey and go out there looking for them?"

Craig took another long pull of his beer before answering. "To tell you the truth, that licorice shit we were drinking that night hit me hard."

"The absinthe?" Haven said.

Craig nodded. "That, and I had a couple of beers too. I don't know if anybody noticed. Hell, even I didn't really notice until we were all out there stumbling around after Elise in the weeds, looking for that damned well. But whatever's in that crap—"

"It's just alcohol," Pierce said.

Craig nodded. "Well, that was enough. It kicked my ass. I mean, Elise had me totally convinced. I wanted to find that stupid well as much as she did. I kept thinking it'd help my dad close a few open cases. We'd be heroes, you know? But I felt like crap. I was so relieved when Haven suggested we give up looking. All I wanted to do was lie down."

Haven thought back to that night. He didn't remember Craig acting particularly intoxicated. Then again, Haven had split his attention that night between Elise and Pierce. He hadn't bothered to think about Craig much at all.

"So the four of us went back to the house," Haven prodded. "Then what?"

Craig's cheeks started to turn a bit red. "Well..." He rubbed his hands roughly over his face. "I mean, come on. We were all horny kids. You know why we were there. Besides for that stupid séance, I mean. And Linsey..." He glanced at Haven. "Well, she was anxious, I guess you could say. We'd only had sex a couple of times, always sort of rushed in the back seat of my car. So she was all worked up over this chance to spend the whole night together. But the thing is"—here, his cheeks began to turn red—"I couldn't do it."

"You couldn't have sex?" Pierce asked, clearly confused as to what any of this had to with the story.

Craig made a snorting sound that was half laughter, half embarrassment. "I was drunk, all right? I couldn't get it up. Hell, I couldn't even see straight. The room was spinning like crazy. All I wanted to do at that point was pass out, but I was too embarrassed to tell Linsey. So I sort of, you know, fumbled through with my hands enough to make her happy. The truth is, we were both lucky I made it through without tossing my cookies right there in the sleeping bag. By the time we finished, I knew those cookies were coming up, one way or another. But I was still too embarrassed to tell Linsey the truth, so I made up some story about looking for Elise."

"But you weren't looking for Elise at all?" Haven asked.

"No. I just went outside to be sick."

"You told Linsey you heard voices, but you never actually heard anything at all?" Pierce asked.

Craig chuckled, looking between the two of them. "Oh, I heard something all right," he said, not unkindly. "When I went past your room." Haven's cheeks immediately turned hot, but Craig just shrugged. "Kind of funny, in hindsight. I'd been raised with this idea that every gay person in the world lived in either Chicago or San Francisco. Never really occurred to me until that night that geography had nothing to do with it."

Haven was too embarrassed to say anything. Pierce only laughed. "We thought we were being so quiet too."

"Well, if I'd been occupied with Linsey the way I should have been, it wouldn't have mattered. But that damned absinthe…"

"You never told anybody," Haven said. "Even with all the questions flying around. You never outed us."

Craig shrugged again. "I couldn't quite see how it mattered. Maybe if that night had gone the way it was supposed to, and Elise hadn't disappeared, it would have been a bigger deal to me. But once we realized Elise was missing…"

"Okay," Pierce said, holding up a hand. "Back up. So, you went outside to get sick. Then what? Did you see my brother and Elise?"

Craig shook his head. "No. But you got to understand, I wasn't exactly looking. I was too busy puking my guts out." He glanced at his half-full beer, but it was as if the talk of being drunk had taken away his urge to drink. "I don't know how long I was out there. I'd throw up, then lie down in the grass and sort of doze for a few minutes. Then I'd have to throw up again, and then I'd lie there with my head pounding."

"You must have been freezing," Haven said. "It was pretty chilly that night."

"Yeah, that too. I didn't know if I was shivering from the cold or because of the puking. All I could think was, Jesus, if there's a ghost here, I hope he'll come get me. Just put me out of my misery." He laughed, leaning back in his chair. "He didn't, though. I just kept on heaving until my stomach ached, and in those little breaks in between where I'd manage to sleep a bit, I kept dreaming about the well. Like we were still looking for it. Like my brain just couldn't let it be."

"Eventually you went back to your car," Pierce said.

"Yeah. Something woke me up, in the middle of one of my little naps between bouts of throwing up. I didn't know what it was. In hindsight, I think it might have been Elise and Jordan going by, but at the time, I couldn't say. But I thought,

I can't go back up to Linsey, because if I need to throw up again, I won't make it all the way down the stairs. I didn't exactly want to sleep there on the ground all night either. So I thought I'd go to my car. I could turn on the heater and lie in the back seat and at least be a bit more comfortable. And I must not have been too far behind Jordan and Elise, because I heard his car start when I was almost back to where we'd parked. My first thought was, 'Those fuckers! They're going home to sleep in their nice, comfortable beds while I'm out here, choosing between the hard ground or my cramped back seat!' And then I realized, hell, I could go home too. So I did."

"Even though you were drunk," Haven said.

"I ain't saying it was the smart choice," Craig conceded. "But the idea of sleeping it off in my own bed was too good to pass up. I figured I'd be able to sneak in, take an Alka-Seltzer, get a couple of hours of sleep, and make it back out to the house by dawn. But it turned out my dad was home." He sat forward again, and reclaimed his beer, although he didn't take a drink. "He was on duty that night, but he'd stopped at the house to refill his Thermos. When he saw me, and realized how drunk I was, he went through the roof. Wanted to know where I'd been and what I'd done. And somehow, between the alcohol and that damn séance, all I could talk about was the stupid well, and how we had to find it. I can't say it makes sense now, but I just had this feeling that if we found the well, and found those missing girls like Elise had said, it wouldn't matter that we'd broken into the house. But all my dad heard was that a cop's kid had broken half a dozen laws, and if anybody found out, his ass'd be grass."

He finally took another drink of his beer, although he didn't seem to relish it the way he had before his story.

"That's it," he said. "My dad grounded me for life and told me to go to bed. I crashed. Next thing I knew, Linsey was calling to say Elise was missing."

For a minute or two, they all sat there in silence, lost in their thoughts. For his part, Haven was still a bit stunned that Craig had kept his and Pierce's secret. He'd come out to his parents three years later. They'd taken it pretty well, but he wasn't so sure they would have handled it with the same good grace when he was seventeen.

Pierce drew Haven's attention by sitting forward, his elbows on his knees. "The thing we keep coming back to," Pierce said, "is that damned well. How the hell did Elise know about it?"

Craig shrugged, clearly uninterested in the question. "Your guess is as good as mine." His eyes went to Haven. "What about you?" he asked. "I know you always blamed Jordan."

"I did. Not anymore."

"So what changed your mind?"

Haven exchanged a look with Pierce, but realized Pierce was only part of his explanation. Craig didn't know about Lance Gustafson.

It only took a few minutes to explain what they'd found out. By the time they finished, Haven could see the excitement and curiosity burning in Craig's eyes. He sat forward, elbows on knees, mirroring Pierce. "So he was the last one to see her that night! And it was his property." He pointed at Pierce. "You're right, though. The real question is, did he tell her about the well?"

It was a question Haven and Pierce had forgotten to ask during Lance's interview. It seemed like it was time to remedy that omission.

CHAPTER 19

Twelve Years Ago

Haven's parents drove him home from the police station in silence, giving him those same strange, lingering looks that hinted at both relief and guilt. They were glad their child wasn't the one missing, but they couldn't help blame Haven and Linsey and their friends for what had happened. He knew they wondered how different things might have been if the group hadn't split up after searching for the well. Haven wondered the same thing himself, every single night.

If only they'd all agreed to sleep together in the living room. Then Elise might never have demanded Jordan take her home. But Haven had been so determined to spend an hour or two alone with Pierce. He'd traded his cousin's life for an hour of sexual experimentation with another boy. It made him feel wretched and selfish, but it wasn't as if anybody had explained it to him ahead of time. There hadn't been any reason to assume his choice would have dire consequences.

Still, no matter how bad he felt, there was nothing to be done about it now. Nothing to do but wait and hope and maybe pray, if Haven could only make himself believe it might help. Every night, Haven dreamed of the Gustafson house. Every night, he searched room after room, calling Elise's name.

After returning home from the police station, Haven knew he'd dream about the house again. Still, he couldn't stay awake forever. He eventually climbed into bed, almost afraid to fall asleep.

Knock, knock, knock.

The rap against his bedroom window was faint, and Haven jumped, his mind immediately going to Cassie Kennedy and Joseph Gustafson. There must be a ghost outside his window! But the very next moment, the knocking came again, a bit harder, and Haven breathed a sigh of relief, chuckling at his own foolishness.

He pushed back the curtain to find Jordan and Pierce on the other side.

Haven threw the lock and slid the window up, out of the way. He caught his reflection in the glass as he did so—skinny and pale, his dark hair a mess, wearing only his briefs—and had a moment of mortification that Pierce was seeing him like this.

"Get dressed and meet us out front," Jordan said. "Hurry!"

They disappeared, scurrying through the thick bushes that mostly hid Haven's window from the street. He only debated for a moment. Anything was better than just lying in bed, knowing the dreams were coming.

Less than five minutes later, he removed the screen from his window and climbed through. He found the twins, along with Linsey and Craig, waiting by Jordan's car, which sat idling at the curb. Linsey and Craig seemed to be doing their best not to look at one another.

"What the hell are you guys doing here?" Haven asked.

It was Jordan who answered. "We have to find the well."

"Are you crazy?" Haven asked. "If we couldn't find it before, how would we find it now?"

"Look, the police refuse to take us seriously. But we know there's something in that well. We know—"

"You don't know anything! We don't even know if the well exists, let alone that there are bodies down it."

"Even if there are," Linsey said, "who cares? My sister won't be down there."

"How do you know?" Craig asked, glaring at her. "If whatever was in that house got to her—"

"There was nothing in that house but us!" Haven protested.

Craig turned on him. "That's bullshit, and you know it. That wasn't Elise's voice we heard during the séance. Something else was out there. If Joseph's ghost managed to kill those farm workers, there's no reason he couldn't have killed Elise too, and done to her what he did to them. He tossed her down the well."

He stopped, as if he'd suddenly run out of gas. The words triggered Haven's memory. Linsey had said she'd heard voices in the house, but when he and Pierce had gone looking, they hadn't found anybody. Had she actually heard anything, or was it only her imagination?

They'd probably never know.

"The well is the key to this whole thing," Jordan said. He looked at Craig, giving him a supportive nod. "I agree with Craig. We have to find it. We have to know what's down there."

Haven glanced around at them, weighing his options. Jordan and Craig were determined. Pierce was gazing at Haven with a look that might almost have been pleading. Linsey stood with her head ducked, tears running down her cheeks.

"Linsey?" he asked, reaching out to put his hand on his cousin's back. He felt her body hitch as another muffled sob shook her.

"Could she be there?" she whispered. "Could Elise be in the well?"

Haven didn't think so, but he heard the note of desperation in her voice. She wanted so much to be able to hope. Haven said the only thing he could.

"There's one way to find out."

They all piled into one car. Haven squished into the middle of the back seat between Linsey and Craig, who had gone back to ignoring each other. The ride to the Gustafson house was silent and awkward.

They parked the car in the same spot. Jordan popped the trunk and produced flashlights, which he handed around to them all. At least this time they were a bit more prepared. He also had a duffle bag, which he threw over his shoulder before slamming the trunk closed.

"Let's do this."

They walked quickly. All of them were a bit out of breath by the time they reached the house. It looked spookier and more ominous than before. They circled it, glancing at it askance, as if it might suddenly pounce.

"We'll do this the right way this time," Jordan said. "We'll spread out in a line." He pointed. "I'll go all the way to the left. Craig, you go all the way to the right. The rest of you, space yourself evenly between us." He turned to point toward the wooded property behind them. "We'll go slow, sort of crossing in a grid, so we cover the ground between us, but always staying even. Got it?"

It made a hell of a lot more sense than just bumbling through the woods in a group as they'd done the first night.

Pierce bumped into Haven as he went past him to his spot in the line, quickly squeezing Haven's hand in the dark, but not saying a word.

And then they started.

Pierce was several yards to Haven's left, his eyes intent upon the ground. Linsey was to his right, sniffling, but uncomplaining. They made their way slowly but surely away from the house.

It was Craig who found the well.

"Here!" he yelled, so suddenly and loudly that Haven jumped. "I think I found it! There's something…"

They all rushed over to Craig, who was bending over in the middle of a tight bunch of bushes, brushing at something on the ground. Haven didn't see anything that looked like a well at all.

"This isn't the ground," Craig was saying, brushing at the dirt. "It's a big board, I think. Like plywood, maybe."

Haven shined his light on the ground, at the place where Craig was uncovering the edge of what did indeed look like plywood.

"That's why we couldn't find it," Craig was saying, moving faster now, brushing who-knew-how-many-years' worth of dirt, leaves, and pine needles aside. "It's just a hole in the ground, and they covered it with this wood..."

With all of them helping, it only took a minute to unearth their find—a large, flat piece of plywood, roughly eight feet square and two inches thick. Craig and Jordan each took a corner, and they lifted it up and away, rotating it over the back edge to reveal a perfectly circular hole in the ground about five feet in diameter.

The smell hit them first.

Haven turned away, fighting the urge to gag. Next to him, Craig dropped his side of the board and made it two steps before vomiting into the brush.

"Jesus, there's something down there for sure," Pierce muttered through his hand, which he held over his nose and mouth. "That's not just water."

"Elise!" Linsey yelled, shining her light down the hole. "Elise, are you down there?"

No sound emerged. They all pointed their flashlights down the well, but all they saw was a faint reflection as the light bounced off the water below.

"I think I see something," Craig said. "Are those sticks?"

"I don't see anything," Haven replied.

"Elise!" Linsey yelled again, frantic now.

But if there was one thing Haven was sure of, it was that Elise wouldn't answer. Even if she was in the well, she obviously wasn't still alive.

He wasn't sure which would be worse—finding her body or not finding her at all.

Jordan dropped his duffle and unzipped it. He pulled out what looked like a long piece of rope tangled with a bundle of straight, flat sticks, just a bit bigger than the kind used to stir paint. He shouldered his way through them all and unrolled the bundle down into the well.

It was a ladder, of sorts. The kind Haven had seen demonstrated at school on fire safety day.

"It's from our room," Pierce explained. "Our bedroom's on the second floor, and my mom's just positive the house is going to burn down one of these days."

"We have to find a place to hook it," Jordan said, pawing at the ground along the edge of the well. Once again, they all bent to brush and dig at the dirt, unearthing the stone ring. Whether or not it had ever been taller, Haven didn't know, but at ground level, the rocks were still in place. The ladder had hooks at the top, meant to be anchored on a windowsill. The rocks served the purpose, although the thought of using it to descend into the depths made Haven's blood run cold.

"Maybe this is a bad idea," Pierce said to his brother as he eyed the flimsy ladder. "I don't think you should climb down there—"

"I'll do it," Haven said, but the twins didn't seem to hear him.

"Just hang on to those hooks," Jordan said to Pierce, slapping him on the shoulder. "If I fall in, I'm blaming you."

There was no good way to hold the hooks, so Craig stood on one, Pierce on the other. Linsey and Haven stood in front of them, a foot or two back from the ring of the well, holding their hands, trying to give them some leverage so they wouldn't tip over backward into the well.

Jordan stuck a flashlight through his belt loop and climbed down.

Haven's palms were clammy as he clung to Pierce's hands. He wished this was something fun and flirtatious rather than utterly horrifying. The twins might pretend it was no big deal, but Pierce couldn't hide his nervousness as his brother descended into the well.

It seemed to take forever. Haven couldn't see anything at all from where he stood. Even Pierce and Craig, standing right on the edge, had their backs to it and couldn't look down the well without craning their necks. It was torture, waiting for Jordan to call up to them, or waiting to hear his scream as he fell. The tension was almost unbearable.

Pierce broke first.

"Jesus Christ, what's taking so long?" he yelled. Despite the callousness of the words, there was no missing the worry in his voice. "Haven't you reached the bottom yet?"

"Hold your horses!" Jordan's voice echoed up from the well. "Almost there." A second ticked by. Then another and another. "We'll have to tell dad that fire or not, this ladder sure as hell won't offer us a quick escape from anything! The rope is slippery and the steps keep twisting under my feet."

Pierce closed his eyes, gripping Haven's hands harder, muttering under his breath. Haven wondered if he was praying.

"It stinks down here," Jordan said. "I'll tell you that much."

"Do you see anything?" Craig asked.

"Hell no. It's pitch dark. I can't see an inch past my face." Another few tense, silent moments. Finally Jordan said, "Okay, I'm at the bottom of the ladder. I think the water is just below me. Hang on. I have to get my flashlight out."

Haven imagined Jordan trying to secure one arm around the rope ladder while pulling the flashlight from his belt loop. The tiny *click* as he flicked it on was surprisingly loud.

Pierce and Craig both twisted, trying to see down to where Jordan was. Haven resisted the urge to rush to the edge to look down with them, because he knew Pierce was counting on him for balance. Next to him, Linsey had her head down, but in the dark, Haven couldn't see her face.

Jordan's voice, when it came again, was low and eerie. "Holy shit."

"What is it?" they all yelled at once. "What do you see?"

"Oh my God," Jordan said. Then again, more fervently, "Oh my God!"

"Is it Elise?" Linsey yelled. "Is it my sister?"

"Jesus!" Jordan said. Then there was nothing but scrambling sounds as he climbed to the top, emerging into the open air far more quickly than he'd descended. He stumbled a few steps before leaning over to dry heave into the dirt.

"What was it?" They were all talking at once. "What did you see?" "Was it Elise?"

"There are bodies down there, all right." Jordan wiped his sleeve across his mouth. "At least two. It was hard to tell. But they're not Elise."

This announcement brought only stunned silence for a moment.

Haven remembered the séance, and Elise-who-wasn't-Elise speaking.

Bodies.

Well.

Here.

"It definitely wasn't Elise?" Linsey asked, her voice hushed and quaking. "How can you be sure?"

Jordan shuddered as he stood upright again and turned to face them. "Whoever those people were, they've been down there way longer than a few days."

CHAPTER 20

Present Day

Pierce called Jordan on the way to the car, and then surprised both Haven by swinging by their motel to pick him up. Haven was in the passenger seat, so Jordan climbed into the back. He and Craig nodded at each other, but didn't say a word as they headed toward the highway. It reminded Haven of the night they'd gone to find the well—of the way Linsey and Craig hadn't spoken the entire ride, while Haven had been stuck between them.

The drive to Altoona would take less than thirty minutes, but having silence the whole would make things damned uncomfortable.

Craig must have thought the same thing, because he eventually cleared his throat nervously. "Haven, I'm sorry we've never made any progress on Elise's case."

"It's fine." It wasn't, though. Not really. But Haven didn't blame Craig.

"I've looked at it myself a couple of times, but there just isn't much to go on. So many people have moved away, and it's not like we can talk to the families of the missing orchard workers. I mean those particular families aren't even around, and the ones who might remember hate talking to the cops. They always pretend like they don't understand English."

"It's fine," Haven said again. But the thought of those missing girls troubled him. It took him a moment to realize why. "Wait a minute," he said, turning in his seat so he could better see Craig's face. "Have there been others?"

"What do you mean?"

"Well, whoever killed those girls was never caught—"

"Or he *was* caught, then found not guilty," Pierce added.

Haven acknowledged the interruption with a nod. "Right. It's possible Lance really is guilty. But either way, the fact is, the killer's still out there. And if I've learned anything from TV, it's that serial killers rarely stop killing."

Jordan nodded, seeing where he was going. "So, you're saying if he's still in the area, other girls must have gone missing." He turned to Craig. "Have they?"

Craig frowned, thinking. "Not from Hobbsburg, no."

"From the migrant camps?" Jordan asked.

Craig's frown deepened. "There was one a few years ago from a camp down by Osterburg, but there's no reason to believe she was ever up this way."

"Anybody else?" Haven asked.

"No…" He sounded more thoughtful than sure though, his gaze going unfocused as he considered the question. "Well," he said after a moment. "Maybe."

"Maybe?" Haven prodded. "What does that mean?"

"There was a girl from Portage who disappeared. She was last seen hitchhiking on 164. Her friends said she was going to Roaring Spring to meet a boy, but she never showed up."

Haven looked at Pierce, whose eyes were on the road. Hobbsburg was on 164, right in between Portage and Roaring Spring.

"That sounds like it qualifies to me," Jordan said.

"She left a note on her bed," Craig said. "That's the thing. Her parents found it the next morning. It was kind of vague. Like, maybe she was just saying goodbye because she was running away. But some people thought she was doing more than that. She had a history of depression."

"So you think she committed suicide?" Haven asked.

Craig shrugged, looking uncomfortable. "I don't know. I'm not saying I bought it. I'm just saying that was one of the options we considered."

Haven thought it sounded like a good excuse for not bothering with a real investigation, but opted to keep his mouth shut.

The navigational system in Pierce's rental car led them to a ranch-style house in a quiet, well-maintained neighborhood of Altoona. Haven couldn't help but wonder, as he climbed from the car, how many of Lance Gustafson's neighbors knew he'd been tried for multiple homicides. It couldn't be an easy thing to live with, even if he had been acquitted.

"Here goes nothing," Jordan mumbled as he rang the bell.

Haven thought Lance would be surprised to see them. He certainly didn't expect any kind of warm welcome. But all his former teacher did was sigh heavily.

"I had a feeling I hadn't seen the last of you yet." He eyed them each in turn. "No cameras?"

"No cameras," Pierce confirmed. "We just want to ask you a few questions."

"Well, at least you showed up while my wife's working." He held the door open for them. "Come on in."

He led them down a hallway lined with pictures of his kids. There seemed to be one boy and one girl. In the course of a few yards, Haven watched them grow from bright-eyed toddlers to young adults. The girl played soccer. The boy played piano and chess.

There were no pictures of Lance or his wife, and Haven had to wonder at that.

Was it possible Lance's wife had known about the affair? Was it possible she'd been the one to follow Elise home? Maybe she'd decided to deal with the home wrecker her own way.

"Your kids are in college now?" Haven asked.

"Yep. One's a junior and one's a freshman. I can't believe how quiet the house is with them gone." He chuckled. "I can't believe I miss the noise, to be honest." He led them to the family room and gestured to the burgundy leather couch and loveseat. Haven found himself sandwiched between the twins on the former as Craig took the latter. Lance sank into a worn recliner, facing them across the biggest coffee table Haven had ever seen.

"Well," he said, "what is it you want to know?"

They all exchanged glances. Haven wanted to ask about Lance's wife—to see if she'd gone anywhere that night. But if she had, it meant Lance had lied about it twelve years earlier. What was to stop him from lying again? Haven glanced at the twins, wishing they'd come up with a plan in the car.

Pierce spoke up first. "You said Elise had sort of a morbid fascination with the house—that she asked a lot of questions about it, and about your brother and Cassie."

Lance winced at the mention of Joseph. "That's right."

"And you eventually told her to cool it, but at first, you must have talked about it a bit."

"Not much, really. I was never anxious to discuss those things."

"But do you remember exactly what you told her?" Pierce asked. "Do you remember if—"

"Did you tell her about the well?" Jordan interrupted. "That's what we need to know. Did you ever tell her about the well?"

Lance shook his head. "I don't think so, no. I don't know why I would have. It wasn't something that ever came up. Not until after…" He blanched. "You know."

"After we found the bodies in it?"

Lance's nod was stiff.

The brothers looked at each other, having one of their silent fraternal dialogs. They both seemed to come up blank, but Haven thought he saw a way forward.

"Let me ask you this," he said, sitting forward in his seat. "Did *you* know about the well? I mean, before Elise disappeared?"

"Yes," Lance said, "but only in theory."

"What the hell does that mean?" Craig asked, speaking for the first time.

Lance sighed heavily, turning to face him. "We went over all of this during my trial, and I was acquitted. You can't question me again. Not without my lawyer."

"You don't need a lawyer," Craig said. "I'm not here as a cop, and this isn't an official investigation."

"Besides, the rest of us weren't at your trial," Jordan said, gesturing to Haven and his brother, including them all in his proclamation. "We were in college at the time, so we have no idea what was said."

"You can't be tried again anyway," Pierce added. "Like you said, you've already been acquitted. So it doesn't really matter what you tell us now, does it?"

Lance scowled. "I didn't hurt Elise." For the first time since their arrival, he seemed angry. "I didn't hurt those other girls, either."

"We believe you," Haven said. He wasn't sure if he had any right speaking for the others, but he needed Lance to stop being defensive and start talking to them. "We're just trying to figure out how Elise might have known about the well."

He waited. It took a moment, but Lance's shoulders finally slumped in defeat. "What do you want to know?"

"Tell us what you mean when you say you only knew about the well in theory?"

"I knew the house had a well, but I'd never been there. I'd never actually seen it. I couldn't have told you where on the property it was located."

"But *how* did you know about it?" Haven asked. "Did your parents mention it?"

"No. Not my parents. It was after Cassie Kennedy was killed. It was—" He stopped short, his eyes going wide. "Oh my God."

"What?" the brothers prompted in unison.

Lance's eyes flicked side to side as he thought back. "It was Joseph."

"Joseph told you about the well?" Haven asked.

Lance shook his head. "Not exactly, no."

He was obviously caught in a memory. Haven tried not to squirm with his impatience as Lance gathered his thoughts.

"I heard it from Joseph," Lance said at last, "but not because he told me." He scrubbed his hands through his hair and sat forward a bit. "You have to realize, I was only nine when Cassie died. And it all happened so fast. She was found on Monday. By Wednesday they were questioning my brother. By Friday he was dead. Those five days felt like…like…" He held up his hands, his eyes on the ceiling, as if hoping to spot and capture the word he needed. "Have you ever seen the Tower card in a tarot deck? The castle destroyed by lightning? That's how it felt. Our whole lives were shattered."

"I can imagine," Haven said quietly. He knew how quickly a normal life could devolve into a nightmare.

Lance nodded, his gaze on the coffee table between them. "My parents tried to protect me. They tried to keep me out of it, but Joseph was my big brother. He was the person I most looked up to. Everybody remembers him as this total screw up, but he wasn't. He didn't have a lot of friends because he was shy. He was…a bit lost, I think. In hindsight, I think—" He stopped short and shook his head, suddenly unwilling to say more.

"You think what?" Haven prodded.

Lance's cheeks turned red. "I think he was in love."

"With Cassie?"

"No. With another boy."

Haven couldn't help but exchange a glance with Pierce.

"Who was it?" Pierce asked.

"I don't know. I only know he had a friend. He'd sneak out at night to see him. He wouldn't ever tell me who he was, but the way he talked about him... "

"You think they were lovers?" Haven said.

Lance pursed his lips. "I doubt it. Not in the way you mean, at rate. But you have to realize, I didn't think any of this at the time. I was too young. All I knew back then was that he was sneaking out to meet a friend."

"But you've had a lot of years to think about it," Haven said.

"Too many. And after teaching high school kids for as long as I have, I feel like I know young love when I see it." Haven didn't doubt it one bit. "Physically, I doubt the relationship was as serious as you probably think, but I'm pretty sure my brother had fallen hard for somebody. All anybody remembers now is that he was weird—that he smoked and got caught drinking. As if every other teenager doesn't do those things. All they remember is the bad stuff. But I'm telling you, my brother wasn't a bad kid. He was just..." He made grasping motions with his fingers as he tried to find the right word. "Trying to figure out who he was."

Haven nodded. Being gay in the early 80s would have been a lot harder than it had been for Haven more than twenty years later. But he could tell by the way Jordan suddenly sat forward that he was getting impatient.

"So Joseph told you about the well?" Jordan asked.

Lance shook his head, pinching the bridge of his nose. "Like I said, I was only nine. It's all a bit hazy. I'll tell you what I remember though. The chief of police came to talk to Joseph on Wednesday." He glanced at Craig. "Not your dad. I mean Lawrence Daavettila."

"My dad wasn't a cop yet," Craig said. "That happened a year or two later."

Lance nodded, already moving on. "My parents sent me up to my room, so I never knew what they talked about. And after it was over, nobody would tell me anything. But they were scared. I knew that much. My brother was sick to his stomach. I mean *literally* sick to his stomach. He went into the bathroom and heaved for the longest time. I remember how pale and shaky he was when he came back out. My mother was in tears. My father could barely look at him. On Thursday, when the police came back a second time, my parents sent me to my room again. But this time..." His hands shook as he pushed his thinning hair back off his forehead. "I snuck downstairs to listen." The room was perfectly still and quiet as they waited for him to go on. "They asked about the key. Joseph said he'd taken it, but that he didn't have it anymore. He said he must have lost it, or that somebody stole it—"

"Sounds familiar," Jordan mumbled.

"They kept asking why he'd killed Cassie, and he kept telling them he hadn't done it. He was getting so angry, because they weren't listening to him. And then..." He sat forward, leaning toward them. "He finally snapped. He told them that if he'd killed Cassie Kennedy, he wouldn't have been stupid enough to leave her lying there where anybody could find her. Joseph said if he'd been the one to kill her, he would have dumped her body down the well, and nobody ever would have found her."

There it was—the thing they'd been waiting to hear. They all drew air at once, each of them reeling backward from the pronouncement.

Pierce recovered first. "Did you ever tell that story to Elise?"

"Not that I remember, but could I swear to it?" Lance shook his head. "It's been so many years. I couldn't say for certain."

"What happened after that?" Jordan asked. "After Daavettila talked to your brother, I mean."

"I stayed up late. When I heard Joseph sneaking downstairs, I followed him. I stopped him before he went out the door. It was the last time I ever saw him." He stopped for a moment, covering his eyes with one hand. They waited, not wanting to push him too hard as he remembered. "He'd been crying, I knew that much. I asked where he was going. I said maybe he should stay in, with everything that had happened. But he said he had to go. He said his friend had a lot of explaining to do." Lance's voice shook as he described the last few minutes he'd ever have with the brother he loved so much. "And that was it," he said at last. "The next day, he wasn't in his bed. He hadn't come home. They found him later that morning, hanging in that horrible house."

"Did the cops ever find out about this friend?" Haven asked.

Lance shook his head. "I told my parents, but I think they figured it didn't matter. He'd left a note. He confessed to killing Cassie. They just wanted to forget the whole thing."

"Mr. Gustafson," Haven said, feeling like the man at least deserved the respect they'd once shown him as a teacher. "What do you think? Do you think your brother killed Cassie?"

Lance's expression was hard to interpret, but Haven thought there was a bit of gratitude in it. "No. I've never believed he was a killer."

CHAPTER 21

Twelve Years Ago

They found three bodies in the well. Haven and his friends had, of course, been sent home, chastised despite their discovery, to wait for the grown-ups to do their thing. After that, the facts seemed to trickle in.

Three bodies, all females in their early twenties, all presumed to be the missing women from the migrant worker camp.

Because of the condition of the bodies, and the environment of the closed-up well, it was hard to say for sure how long they'd been dead, but the coroner estimated that the first one had gone in approximately fifteen years earlier, with the next two coming at five-year increments. It was only an estimate, but the press ran with it as if it were gospel. An article in the newspaper speculated that if this was a serial killer, the next body was due to be dropped down the well that very year.

Which, of course, led to Elise.

Whoever had killed those women must have murdered Elise as well. And yet, if he did, why hadn't she been found there, along with the others?

Theories abounded, but Haven had his own.

The bodies in the well were a coincidence. Whether Elise had somehow made a lucky guess, or whether it had really

172

been Cassie speaking to them didn't matter. The first of those women had been killed when Haven and his friends were still in diapers, so it was clear none of them were the killer. And despite what Jordan and Craig seemed to think, Haven knew it wasn't a ghost who'd taken Elise from them. He didn't think it was whoever had killed the migrant workers either. After all what were the odds that their resident serial killer had just happened to stumble across Elise that very night as she made her way home?

Almost nil.

The more Haven thought about it over the next few weeks, the more certain he became. Somebody in their group had killed Elise.

Of the five of them, only one had a reason.

Jordan.

But for better or worse, Jordan had been all but eliminated as a suspect. Everybody seemed to assume Elise had been taken by the man who'd killed the migrant workers. The focus shifted away from the kids who'd been at the house that night and toward some unknown perpetrator.

Haven's certainty that Jordan was guilty grew every day. The more he thought about it, the more logical it seemed. He began to dream of the day the police would come to the obvious conclusion and make their arrest. But this wasn't like *Law & Order* or *CSI*, where the killer was found and brought to justice in an hour. The wheels of the law turned at a frustratingly slow pace.

The night before the twins were due to leave for college, Pierce knocked on Haven's front door. Haven's stomach twisted into a painful knot at the sight of him. Not so long ago his reaction would have only been excitement and nervous attraction. Now it was tainted with bitterness and rage.

"Can you come out for a minute?" Pierce asked, his cheeks red. "I thought we could talk."

Haven's parents were both at work. He could invite Pierce in, but the thought turned him cold. He was about to tell Pierce no, he didn't want to talk to him at all when Pierce said, "Please?"

Haven sighed, feeling weak and pathetic. He stepped outside, closing the front door behind him. He didn't take another step though. He crossed his arms, wishing he could hate Pierce as much as he hated Jordan, wishing he didn't still want more than anything to spend every waking minute in his presence. "What do you want?"

Pierce blinked in surprise. "I didn't want to leave without saying goodbye."

Goodbye. The word was so heavy and loaded and final. It almost brought tears to Haven's eyes.

"Haven." Pierce stepped closer and put his hand on Haven's arm. "I know this is all screwed up. I know everything's gone wrong, but it doesn't mean anything has to change between us. It doesn't mean we can't still be friends. Or…well." His red cheeks darkened, but he didn't look away. "Maybe we can even be more than friends, you know?"

God, how Haven would have loved to hear Pierce say those words before that awful night had turned his entire life upside down. Haven forced himself to speak. "I don't think that's a good idea."

Pierce's eyebrows came together in a mixture of hurt and confusion that nearly broke Haven's resolve. "I thought we felt the same way. I thought—"

"Not anymore."

"But—"

"Jordan killed Elise. You know that, right?"

"No." Pierce shook his head. "He didn't. I swear he didn't. I can see why you'd think that, but I promise you—"

"Save it." Haven hated the way his voice cracked on the words. "He's your twin brother. Of course you're going to lie for him."

"I'm not lying."

"Then where is she?" His voice was louder than he intended, shaking with anger and confusion and the effort of holding back tears. "Where is she, if he didn't kill her?"

"Haven, I don't know. If I knew anything, I'd tell you. I'd tell the police. I'd—"

"Not if it meant getting your brother arrested. Not if it meant admitting he's a killer!"

Pierce's face hardened into something Haven had never seen on it before. "Jordan only gave her a ride. He didn't hurt her. He—"

"He was pissed because she wouldn't put out! Did he rape her first? Is that what happened? Then he had to kill her so she wouldn't tell? Or was he so mad that he killed her before he could follow through?"

"Haven—"

Haven lunged forward, shoving Pierce hard in the chest with both hands. "I want to know what he did to her!"

Haven's push knocked Pierce back a step. Haven wondered if he'd come back swinging. He almost hoped he would. If Pierce hit him, it'd be easier to stop liking him so much. It'd be easier to walk away and pretend he'd never cared about Pierce at all.

But Pierce made no move to strike him. He wasn't the kind of guy who resorted to using his fists. He crossed his arms and ducked his head. Haven waited, his heart pounding, thinking maybe Pierce would finally admit that he'd realized Jordan was the obvious culprit too. Maybe Pierce would somehow still be able to make everything right.

Pierce took a deep steadying breath. Then another. He reached slowly into his back pocket and pulled out a folded piece of paper. He held it out to Haven, his hand shaking. "Take it. Please."

"What is it?"

"It's my address at Ohio State." Haven was surprised to hear that Pierce's voice was as strained as his own had been. "I was going to ask you to keep in touch. I was hoping we could—" He stopped, swallowing hard. His hand shook harder, causing the paper to rattle. "Maybe you'll feel different in a week or two. Maybe once they find out what happened—"

"No." It was the hardest word Haven had ever spoken. His eyes began to fill with tears, but he wiped them angrily away. "I already know what happened. And I don't ever want to see you again." God, if only those words were actually true, it would have made this so much easier.

Pierce's hand fell to his side, his shoulders falling in defeat. "Haven, please…"

"Go to hell," Haven said, turning to open the door. He needed to get away before he lost it completely. "Take your murdering brother with you."

He shut the door before Pierce could protest. And if he cried when Pierce finally drove away, at least nobody was there to see it.

An enormous chain-link fence went up around the Gustafson property a few days later, ensuring that no more teenagers snuck inside. Tales of ghosts seen on the property by the friend of a friend on some long-ago, unspecified night, skyrocketed. Once school started, Haven couldn't go a week without hearing a new one. Only now his cousin's spirit was said to walk the grounds too. At least one person claimed they'd seen Elise through one of the upstairs windows. Haven knew they were lies. The new fence meant they couldn't get within fifty yards of the place.

Tips continued to trickle in from other cities as well. People all over the state, and as far away as Wyoming, reported sightings of a woman who looked like Elise. Some said she was homeless. Some said she looked happy and healthy. One even claimed she'd joined a nearby cult. None of them panned out. Some people still believed she might be out there somewhere, living her life in secret. Haven knew in his heart they were wrong.

A few months after the Hunter brothers left, when Haven was halfway through his senior year of high school, the police arrived midway through AP English to take Lance Gustafson away in handcuffs. They charged him with the murders of the women whose bodies had been found in the well, and assured Elise's family that if he was found guilty, he'd be charged separately with Elise's kidnapping. But it wasn't to be. The evidence was all circumstantial, the entire case hinging on the fact that he owned the property. He'd eventually be acquitted, at which point, he and his family would quickly relocate to a town where their names weren't instantly connected to a well full of death.

But by that point Haven had graduated from high school, his eyes already set on college.

He missed his cousin more than he ever could have imagined, but he knew she was dead. The police said the investigation was ongoing, but Haven knew they thought the killer, Lance Gustafson, had already walked free.

Haven knew her real killer was actually a student at Ohio State.

Sometimes, in that shadowy place between wakefulness and sleep, Haven dreamed of the night he'd once spent in a dark, cold room, exploring his newfound sexuality with a boy he could have grown to love. He replayed that last conversation with Pierce, wondering what might have been. Sometimes he wanted nothing more than to reach out to Pierce and try to make things right. Other times, he refused to acknowledge that he'd ever cared about Pierce at all.

He knew he'd see Pierce Hunter again someday.

The only question was when.

CHAPTER 22

Present Day

They were quiet as Pierce drove them back to Hobbsburg, each lost in his own thoughts.

Craig seemed tense, his knee bouncing incessantly as he stared moodily out the window. Haven thought he caught Pierce and Jordan exchanging weighted glances in the rearview mirror, but could only guess at their meaning. As for himself, Haven was hung up on Lance's story.

He was stuck on the thought of Joseph.

Maybe the abandoned house had been Joseph's hideaway. If he'd been sneaking out to meet somebody there, it was possible he'd given that person the key. It was also possible this "friend" had simply taken it, the way Elise had apparently taken Lance's.

But once Cassie died, everything would have changed. Joseph must have suspected his friend of Cassie's murder, yet he'd kept it to himself. He'd protected his friend, even though it made him look like the only feasible suspect in Cassie's murder. It seemed like a big risk to take for a mere acquaintance. But for somebody he was in love with? Maybe not.

Had this friend loved him back? For some reason, Haven wanted to believe he did. But if so, why would he have raped and killed Cassie Kennedy? Unless they'd killed her

178

together. Or maybe there was a third party involved whom nobody had thought of yet. Haven wished he could ask Pierce his opinion, but he was reluctant to do it with the others in the car.

Besides, whatever had happened with Cassie, it seemed unrelated to Elise. If it'd been the same killer, her body would have been in the well with the others.

So maybe it was Lance after all.

Or Lance's wife.

Or maybe...

Haven glanced over his shoulder at Craig, whose jaw was clenched tight.

Was it possible?

It wasn't until they'd dropped Craig off at his home that Pierce turned to his brother and said, "You got all that, right?"

The question confused Haven until Jordan pulled something from his pocket and held it up. It was one of the handheld digital recorders they often used on the show to capture EVPs.

"I recorded every word."

"Good." Pierce's gaze flicked Haven's way, bringing him into the conversation. "You know what we have to do now."

Jordan laughed. "You happen have an emergency fire ladder with you?"

"No," Pierce said as he put the car into drive, "but I bet they sell them at Walmart."

"We can pick up a couple of flashlights while we're at it."

Haven could only gape at them. "Are you guys serious?"

"Hell yeah, we're serious," Jordan said. "One of us is going back down that well."

Haven felt a dark twinge of déjà vu as they pulled up the Gustafson house. The trucks and production tent had disappeared, leaving the house abandoned once again. The *Paranormal Hunters* crew had packed up and returned to the studio to cobble together their footage into a two-part episode. Pierce and Jordan planned to join them in the next couple of days—or that's how it sounded to Haven, as he listened to them talk—but first, they were determined to put the spirits of the well to rest.

Pierce killed the engine, and the three of them stepped out of the car. The house was a dark silhouette against the dim twilight glow of the western sky. Lightning bugs flitted through the nearby weeds. The overgrown lawn swayed in a faint breeze. Pierce's arm brushed his, although now Haven knew it hadn't been accidental. Once before, he'd stood here next to Pierce, knowing his life was about to change. The feeling came back, as strong as on that distant night. Time seemed to blur and shift, the past meeting the present. He could almost see Elise standing a few feet ahead of him, twirling her keys around her finger. He almost thought he detected her laughter in the rustling of the leaves. Pierce reached over and took his hand, suddenly rooting him solidly in the present.

Suddenly Haven knew—everything was as it was meant to be. This was the beginning of the end.

The house was waiting for them to set things right.

"Light's fading fast," Jordan said, his voice oddly hushed. "I say we get this over with."

At least this time they didn't have to search for the well. Not for long, at any rate, although the bushes around its edge were thicker than ever.

Haven remembered the photo they'd shown him of the well as it had once been—so idyllic and innocent. When had the picturesque roof and bucket disappeared? When had the stone ring come down? When had something that was supposed to give water and life turned into something filled with death?

The sheet of plywood was gone. There was nothing but a dark, deep hole in the earth. The smell was nothing like it had been twelve years earlier. Haven still thought he detected a tinge of rot and decay though. Was it real or only his memory playing tricks?

The twins unrolled the ladder, letting it drop into the well, and secured the hooks on the stone rim.

"This one's better than the one we had before," Pierce said.

"Definitely. Those hooks aren't going anywhere."

They still knelt at the well's edge. Pierce waited until Jordan met his gaze. "I'm going," Pierce said. Not because he wanted to go, Haven knew, but because he couldn't stand to wait on the surface while his brother went down that dark hole again.

It seemed Jordan felt the same way. "Absolutely not."

"You went last time. It's only fair."

Jordan scowled. "Rock, paper, scissors?"

"Fine."

They each held up a fist—

"I'll go," Haven said, the words escaping his mouth before he'd entirely decided to say them.

The twins turned to stare at him, their fists still at the ready, although the waning light made it hard to see their expressions.

"She was my cousin." Haven wished he were steadier. He wished his voice didn't tremble with every word. "I want to be the one to climb down."

The twins turned to each other, doing one of their strange silent exchanges. Haven didn't have to be a mind reader to know Pierce was going to object. He would want to protect Haven from whatever might be down in that dark place, just like he wanted to protect Jordan.

"No—" Pierce started to say.

"Okay," Jordan interrupted. Whether because he understood Haven's need to do it himself or whether he was simply happy to keep himself and his brother safe, Haven didn't know. He figured it didn't matter either way.

"Thank you."

"The ladder's way more secure than it was last time," Jordan assured him. "We won't let you fall."

"I know."

They'd picked up a battery-operated lantern at Walmart. Jordan set it up on a nearby rock. It illuminated a circle roughly six feet in diameter, interrupted here and there by the heavy shadow of bushes and low trees. Haven tested their new flashlight. It was heavy enough to be used as a weapon and bright enough to send a direct beam past the treetops, seemingly halfway to the stars. He hooked it into his belt loop, just as Jordan had done twelve years earlier. His jeans would be riding low on one side by the time he got to the bottom.

He tried not to think about what he might find there.

Pierce's anxiety was almost palpable. His jaw tight, he steadfastly refused to meet anybody's eyes. Haven knew it'd be just as bad if it were Jordan climbing down.

"I'll be fine," Haven said, as much to himself as to Pierce.

Pierce jerked his head in the semblance of a nod, but said nothing. Haven wanted to go to him. As childish as it was, he wanted Pierce to look at him, or hold him, or even kiss him before they took another step, but none of those things seemed feasible with Jordan looking on. He'd only end up feeling like a fool.

Haven took a deep breath to steady himself, then began his descent.

The light of the lantern didn't reach into the well, so Haven climbed down into pitch black. He could hear nothing but the rattle of the ladder against the rocks, the steady pounding of his heart, and the echo of his own labored breathing. He wished he wasn't so scared. Logically he knew he had nothing to fear. It was just a hole in the ground. Whatever was at the bottom—if there was anything there at all besides water—couldn't possibly hurt him. There was no logical reason for his hands to shake; no reason for his heart to pound so violently against his ribs.

Rationalization didn't do much against the blackness though.

"Haven?" Pierce called from above. "Talk to me."

Haven stopped his slow descent, his hands aching as he clung to the ladder. It took two tries to make his voice work. "I'm fine."

He heard Pierce's muffled curse, and then the calm murmur of Jordan's voice, probably telling Pierce to stop freaking out over nothing, although Haven couldn't distinguish the exact words. He remembered holding Pierce's hands as Jordan had climbed into the well. He remembered the way Pierce's lips had moved, as if he were praying.

Haven kept climbing down.

He had renewed sympathy for Jordan, who'd been the first of them to do this. The ladder seemed to go on and on, like some kind of nightmare, growing longer and longer, descending into a surrealistic hell Haven might have written a book about. Elise would have enjoyed the hell out of it. The flashlight swung with each step, bumping against his thigh. He wanted to tug his pants back up into place, but he didn't dare let go of the ladder. The air felt thick and heavy. His lungs didn't seem to collect oxygen the way they were supposed to. Each time his foot moved down, he had to feel around with his toe to find the next board.

Until finally, his toe found nothing.

He groped farther down, then back up, searching for the step. His palms were slippery on the ladder's rope.

Nope. There was no step there. He'd finally reached the end.

"Okay," he called up. "I'm at the bottom. Give me a second."

He hooked one elbow around the ladder, freeing his other hand to pull the flashlight from his belt loop. He flipped it on, then took one more deep, calming breath before aiming its beam downward.

It took him a minute to figure out what he was seeing. The surface of the water lay about two feet below him. It didn't reflect the beam back at him as he'd expected. It seemed to devour the light. It was more like staring down at a thick pit of mud. A few leaves and twigs sat on the surface, but the water itself was dark with moss and God only knew what. Haven was suddenly reminded of Pierce's comment about Loch Ness, how the water was too black to see through. Peat content, Pierce had said, but Haven had no idea whether or not to blame peat this time. He slowly panned the light around the circle of the well, looking for anything that might be a body.

When he found it, he gasped. His stomach roiled and threatened to empty itself.

A large branch had fallen into the well at some point. It stuck up out of the water at an angle, wedged against the wall. Draped across the branch was a dark, horrifying form.

The flesh was mostly rotted, whatever was left of the body coated in something dark and slimy in the light of Haven's flashlight. He squinted, trying to make it all come into focus, and found a row of neat, white, nearly parallel lines.

Ribs.

Haven turned away, fighting the urge to be sick. Whether there were more bodies under the water or not, he had no way of knowing. He needed to climb back up the ladder, get the hell out of the well, and call for help. It was a wonder Pierce hadn't already yelled for him to come back up. He was about to call up, to let them know what he'd found, when a new voice cut through the night.

"I had a feeling I'd find you boys here."

Haven looked up. He could just barely distinguish the dark forms of Pierce and Jordan standing on the edge of the well, backlit by the lantern. But who had found them?

"Chief Fuller," Jordan said, answering Haven's question. "What are you doing here?"

"Craig came down to the station, foaming at the mouth about checking Cassie Kennedy's old case file. Said he needed to know if something Joseph had once said was recorded in there." A couple of seconds ticked by, punctuated by the rapid-fire pounding of Haven's heart. "Where's your writer friend?" Chief Fuller asked.

"We dropped him off at his motel," Pierce said. "I think he went back to Pittsburgh already."

"That's what you two should have done. I told you not to make a spectacle out of this."

"Do you see any crowds?" Jordan asked. "We're the only ones here."

"Have you been down the well yet?"

One silent second ticked by as Haven wondered what they'd say, and then Pierce answered. "Yes. We've seen the bodies. We know you killed them."

Haven leaned his head against the cool stone wall of the well, breathing a sigh of relief. So, Pierce had figured it out as well. The only question now was how to get out of this new mess.

They needed to call for help.

"What makes you think it was me?" Chief Fuller asked.

"That night, twelve years ago," Pierce said. "The night we broke into this house? Craig went home. He told you Elise wanted to look for the well."

"Yeah," Fuller admitted. "So what?"

"You knew she was right," Jordan said. "You knew there were bodies in the well, because you'd put them there."

"Did you panic right then?" Pierce asked. "Or did you figure nobody'd listen to a bunch of trespassing kids anyway?"

Haven didn't want the flashlight beam to give him away. He held his breath and moved the switch as slowly as he could to the "off" position, praying the "click" wouldn't give him away. He slid the flashlight back into his belt loop and reached for the cell phone in his pocket.

"It must have felt like fate when you went back out to finish your shift and happened upon Elise," Jordan said. "She was on her way home from Lance Gustafson's house. Did she tell you that? Did she tell you about their affair? Or did she say she'd been at Judy Roberts's house?"

"I don't know what you're talking about," Chief Fuller said. "You were the last one to see her. Everybody knows you're the one who killed her."

Haven used the switch on the side of his phone to put it in silent mode, then chewed his lip, debating who to call. Dialing 911 would likely get his call dispatched to the local police department. A fat lot of good that would do them. If he had time to look up the number, he figured the State Troopers or the FBI might have been the best bet when dealing with a corrupt cop, but he had no idea how to reach any of them.

"It wasn't Jordan," Pierce said. "It was you. You obviously waited until after the well had been searched before dumping Elise into it. It must have been a tense few days for you, wondering if or when Chief Daavettila would finally check the well. Was Elise alive that whole time, or did you kill her right away?"

"I never killed her at all," Fuller said. "Maybe it was Craig. He left the house that night the same time Jordan and Elise left. How do you know he didn't kill her?"

"Really?" Jordan asked, incredulous. "You're going to throw your own son under the bus to save your sorry skin?"

"I'm only pointing out the hole in your logic."

Haven looked at his phone, scanning the log of the last few calls he'd made.

He chose one and hit dial.

"We know it wasn't Craig," Jordan was saying, "because he's our age. He was only a kid when the first body went down the well."

"Besides," Pierce said, "you were friends with Joseph Gustafson. Craig told us that when we first broke into this house. You probably took the key from him and brought Cassie Kennedy out here to kill her."

"Then, when Joseph confronted you," Jordan took up the tale again, "you killed him, and made it look like a suicide."

"I have no idea what you're talking about."

"Did you kill anybody over those next couple of years?" Pierce asked. "Or did you hold off until you were a cop and you read Cassie's file? Because that's what gave you the idea, right? You saw what Joseph said to Daavettila about tossing the bodies down the well, and suddenly you had the perfect way to get away with murder."

Haven held the phone to his ear, waiting for the call to go through.

"You just said it yourself, son. Chief Daavettila was the one who took that report. He was the one who would have known about the well."

"Except Daavettila had a stroke eight years ago," Pierce said, his voice calm and reasonable, the way he often sounded when debunking Jordan's wild ideas on the show. "He's been in a nursing home since then. True, he could have killed that first set of girls, including Elise. But not the more recent ones."

"Maybe it was Lance Gustafson."

"Lance doesn't even have a key to the gate," Pierce said. "But you probably do. You're the one who had the fence put up in the first place."

"So it isn't Craig," Jordan said, "and it isn't me, and it isn't Lance or Lawrence Daavettila. That only leaves one person. One person who knew Cassie, who knew Joseph, who knew about the well, and who knew that Elise might open a big, ugly can of worms."

"You," Pierce added. "You killed them all."

"Hello?" the voice on the other end of the phone said.

If Haven whispered, would Fuller hear him?

"Hello?" the voice said again. "Is anybody there?"

"I'd only planned to send the two of you on your way," Fuller said, "but I guess desperate times call for desperate measures."

Haven heard two footsteps in the gravel. Pierce gasped. Jordan screamed, "No!"

And then...

BANG!

The sound of the gun echoed around Haven, temporarily deafening him. He looked up in time to see Pierce topple over backward into the well, his limbs splayed against the bright circle of light. He crashed into Haven on his way down, knocking him off the ladder. The phone flew out of Haven's hand before he plunged into the slimy, dark water. It wasn't deep, but it was icy cold, and Haven tried not to gasp.

Tried not to splash.

Tried not to make any sound as he surfaced. He also tried not to think about exactly why it felt so greasy and foul against his skin.

"No!" Jordan screamed. "Pierce!"

"Shut up!" Fuller growled. "Just shut the fuck up, would you?"

"You're just going to shoot me anyway, so why does it matter? It's not like anybody can hear me."

"How would shooting you help me, kid?"

"But—" Jordan gasped for air. "My brother—" He might have been sobbing, but it didn't seem to matter to Chief Fuller.

"You and I are going to the house," he said. "Start walking."

Haven figured Fuller's gun must now be pointed at Jordan. He remained perfectly still, not even straightening the glasses that had been knocked askew on his face, listening to their receding footsteps.

Now what?

Haven took a moment to take stock of the situation. The water was only about two-and-a-half feet deep. It was cold and stinky and slimy. He might have vomited if he hadn't been so scared. The absence of light at the top of the well told him Fuller had taken the lantern. The darkness was a blessing, though. It meant he didn't have to face the worst of the situation yet.

The flashlight still hung heavily from Haven's belt loop. Would it work after being fully submerged? He pulled it free and breathed a sigh of relief when it clicked on, the beam piercing the darkness.

Haven nudged his glasses back into place and steeled himself for what he expected to find.

He had been lucky enough to miss the branch and its gruesome prize when he fell, but Pierce hadn't. The horrible refuse made a morbid sort of ramp, Pierce's body splayed grotesquely across them. His head lay against the side of the well, above the water line, one temple stained with blood. He was mostly submerged from the hips down. The bullet had entered in the place where his right arm met his collarbone, staining the entire front of his shirt with blood.

But his chest moved in a slow, rhythmic pattern.

"Pierce?" Haven whispered, even though he knew Jordan and Chief Fuller had moved away. He put his hand on Pierce's chest and felt his heart beating hard and strong against his palm. "Oh, Jesus, Pierce. Are you all right?"

If Fuller had shot him in the chest, why was his head bleeding? Haven wiped blood away, shining the light on Pierce's skull. He found only an abrasion, and a quickly forming lump. Pierce must have hit his head on the way down.

Pierce groaned and jerked away, startling Haven. "I'm gonna be blind if you keep shining that thing in my eyes."

Haven nearly sobbed with relief, putting his head against Pierce's chest. They were stuck in a freezing cold well filled with rotting corpses. He'd lost his phone. Jordan was gone, at the mercy of a cold-blooded serial killer.

But for now, at least, Pierce was alive.

"Are you okay?" His worst fear now was that Pierce had broken his back when he hit the branch. "Can you move?"

"I think so," Pierce muttered. "Everything seems to still be attached. Thanks for breaking my fall." He shifted, then groaned. "What am I lying on?"

"You don't want to know."

"I was afraid you'd say that."

"We have to get out of here," Haven whispered. "Where's your phone?"

"In my back pocket. Right side." He made a move toward it with his left hand, before subsiding with a groan. "I don't think I can reach it."

"I'll get it."

The back pocket in question lay completely submerged, but maybe his phone would still work. Haven pulled it free, sighing in relief when he saw the protective case. But when he hit the button, nothing happened. He tried again and again, but the result was the same.

"The battery's dead."

"It shouldn't be."

"It is." Haven looked up, eyeing the ladder that still hung down the side of the well. "Do you think you can climb out?"

Pierce shifted, testing his limbs, but didn't get far before he groaned and fell back against his gruesome resting place. "I did something to my ankle. And I can't use my right arm."

"Shit!" Haven turned the beam of the light around and around their wet confines, looking for his cell phone. It'd fallen out of his hand. He couldn't see anything past the dark, oily surface of the water.

"Hold this."

He handed Pierce the light and stooped down, feeling around in the water for his phone. The water came up to his neck, but he was able to keep his head above the surface. His fingers fumbled across rocks, bones, things he didn't want to think about. Then, something distinctly non-organic.

Something metallic.

Something he recognized.

Not his phone, though. He pulled it up, holding his find into the beam of the light. It was a set of keys. The fake jewels on the "Class of '03" key ring still sparkled in the light.

"Looks like we found Elise," Pierce said. His face was ashen in the reflected beam of the flashlight.

"How did you know it was him? And how did you know there were bodies down here?" Haven asked. "I was about to tell you, but he appeared—"

"Lucky guess."

It struck Haven as funny, which also felt horribly wrong. He choked back his laughter and slid the keys into his pocket before resuming his search for the phone. It seemed to take ages, although Haven guessed it was only another thirty seconds or so before he found it. It was dead after being in the water so long. They didn't exactly have time to wait for it to dry out. Pierce's teeth began to chatter. He was going into shock and there wasn't a damned thing Haven could do about it.

He turned the flashlight off, hanging it once more from his belt loop. Pierce could only use one hand, and it was better for him to have the phone than the light. Maybe it'd be functional again quicker than Haven expected. If that happened, he'd be able to call for help.

If not...

Well, Haven hoped to have some other solution in the works by then.

What exactly that solution would be, he had no idea.

He leaned over Pierce, wishing it wasn't so damned dark. "Hang on, you hear me? Don't you dare die down here."

"I'm fine. Go. Don't let him kill my brother."

"I won't."

Haven turned to go, but stopped when Pierce said his name. "Haven. Wait."

He turned back, leaning close. "What is it?"

"You didn't steal the stories. She only planted the seed. You're the one who made them grow."

Haven didn't have time to think through what that meant, or why Pierce felt the need to say it now. He kissed Pierce's forehead. "I'll be back."

"With pizza, I hope. We never did have dinner."

He was glad that, even now, Pierce could joke. "I'll see what I can do."

It was harder than he expected to get back onto the ladder, the end of which was just above his head. It wasn't graceful, but with a bit of work, he managed to hang onto the bottom of the ladder with his hands, brace his feet against the stone wall, and scramble up to the first rung. He worried with each and every step the ladder would slip off the stone rim of the well, and he'd fall, but somehow, it stayed in place.

He finally emerged, soaked and shivering, into the clear, calm night. It was a pleasantly warm evening, but not warm enough to be running around dripping wet. And however bad it was for him, it would be worse for Pierce, who couldn't get all the way out of the water and couldn't move around enough to keep his blood pumping.

The lantern was gone, but the forest seemed unnaturally bright after the darkness of the well. The moon had risen while he'd been deep in the earth. It was damn near full and illuminated the forest with a pale, silvery glow. Haven glanced down once, wanting to see Pierce again—wanting to have one last word of encouragement—but the bottom of the well was lost to darkness.

He was wasting time. Saving Pierce wouldn't be worth much if he lost Jordan in the bargain. Pierce would never be able to forgive him for that.

Haven ran toward the house, panting a prayer in time with his steps. *Let Pierce live. Let Pierce live. Let Pierce live.*

It seemed strange that the house still stood unmoving and uncaring while his world fell to pieces. Fuller's car sat next to Pierce's rental. Haven ran to it, hoping to use the radio. It couldn't be too hard, right? He figured he'd just hit the button and scream for help until somebody answered.

The car door was locked.

Haven turned toward the house and saw the front door stood open. A bit of light glowed from one of the upstairs windows. It was faint, but definitely there.

Haven crept forward, trying to balance speed against silence.

The front room of the house was empty, but a glance up the stairs showed him all he needed to see.

The lantern sat on the upper landing. Chief Fuller stood with his back to Haven. For some reason, Haven expected him to be in his full cop get-up, but he wasn't. He wore jeans. His light green golf shirt was a strange counterpoint to the gun he held pointed at Jordan's head.

Jordan stood at the upper railing of the stairs, tying a rope around the banister. Even from where Haven crouched, hidden in the shadows, he could see the way Jordan's hands shook. He could see the tear stains on his cheeks.

"They'll do ballistics tests. They'll know the bullet in my brother's chest came from your gun."

"This isn't my service weapon, kid. I'm not as stupid as you think."

Haven toed off each of his sodden sneakers to keep them from squishing with every step.

"Is this what you did to Joseph Gustafson?" Jordan asked. "Did you force him to hang himself?"

"No. I strangled him myself, then hung him over the railing. Luckily for me, the coroner back then was burned out and lazy. He was perfectly happy to chalk it up to suicide."

"And the note?"

"I forged it. It wasn't hard. It won't be hard to forge yours either."

Haven took one slow, careful step toward the stairs. He just needed Jordan to keep Fuller talking. He had a feeling that was his plan anyway. Even if Jordan ended up swinging from the railing, even if the new coroner was burned out and lazy too, they sure wouldn't miss the digital recorder in the dead man's pocket. Haven would have bet his last dollar it was recording every word Chief Fuller said.

Haven took another slow, careful step up, keeping his back against the wall.

"You're a cold-hearted bastard," Jordan said. "Did it even matter to you that Joseph loved you?"

Fuller's laugh was full of scorn. "He was gullible. He believed what he wanted to believe."

"And Elise? Where was she?"

"I kept her up in the hills, at my hunting cabin."

"Was she alive the whole time?"

"Only a day or two. I never should've taken her. She was so damned stubborn, she wasn't even any fun. But of course, I had to kill her by that point. I'd just about decided Daavettila wouldn't ever search the well. I planned to dump her body that night, but you and your friends took matters into your own hands, and I had to wait several more days. You definitely caused me a fair bit of trouble."

"Don't expect me to apologize."

Haven took another step. And another. Was it just his imagination, or had Jordan's eyes flicked his way? If they had, it had only been for a fraction of a second.

"Do you really think making me hang myself will solve anything? They'll look for Pierce. They'll check the well—"

"Even if they do, it won't matter. Your note will explain the whole thing."

"It'll explain what, exactly?"

"How Pierce figured out that you killed Elise twelve years ago. He figured out that you've been coming back here, killing girls ever since. So you shot him, then hung yourself out of guilt."

Two more steps. Haven worried with each one the creaky house would betray him, but luck was on his side. He'd nearly reached the top.

"That doesn't even make sense."

"It's a haunted house! It doesn't need to make sense. You, of all people, should know that."

"They'll connect the new bodies to the ones from before. They'll know it couldn't have been me—"

"For fuck sake, kid. Just shut up and get on with it!"

Haven reached the landing, feeling for the flashlight. He slid it slowly from his belt loop, thankful the twins had gone for the heavy-duty Maglite and not some cheap, plastic imitation.

Chief Fuller was only about four feet away.

"What's taking so long? How long does it take you to tie a damned knot?"

"Excuse me if I'm not exactly in a hurry, you psychotic bastard!"

Haven might have laughed if he wasn't so scared. He hefted the flashlight and took one careful step forward.

The floorboard creaked loudly under his foot. Chief Fuller spun toward Haven. All Haven saw was the black barrel of the gun, turning his way.

He lunged forward, swinging the flashlight as hard as he could with both hands. The *bang* it made as it cracked against Fuller's skull was louder than it should have been, knocking Haven back a step.

The Chief fell hard. His pistol skittered across the floor. Jordan dropped the rope and dove for the gun.

Haven landed with a *thump* on his backside, his head spinning, his side aching.

Chief Fuller lay on his back, not moving. Jordan came up with the gun and turned to point it at Fuller. His hands may have been shaking before, but they looked steady enough now.

"Haven, are you okay?"

"I'm fine. I fell. I don't know why I fell."

"You've been shot."

"What?"

"Are you okay?"

Haven looked down at his side. His clothes were still wet from the well, but he was surprised to see a darker stain spreading across his T-shirt.

The pain hit next, stabbing up from his side, almost causing him to scream. He bit it back and swore instead. "Holy Jesus. When did that happen?"

Chief Fuller still hadn't moved, although Haven could see his chest rising and falling. Jordan knelt and patted him down. He must not have found any other weapons, because he stood up and took a step backward, the pistol still leveled at the Chief's head.

Haven found the hole in his side fascinating. It was smaller than he expected, about an inch above the waist of his jeans. Another inch or two to the left, and Fuller would have missed him completely. Haven's back felt warm, and when he slid his hand around his side, he found a matching hole there. "It went right through."

"I ought to kill him," Jordan said, his voice strained and tight. "He'd deserve it for killing Pierce."

"He's not dead," Haven said.

"What? Haven! What did you just say?"

"He's not dead."

"Are you talking about Fuller or Pierce?"

Haven wasn't sure why their conversation was so hard to follow. Maybe it was because he was replaying the last ninety seconds in his head, trying to figure out exactly when he'd been shot. "Both, I guess." If he put his thumb on one of the bullet holes and reached around his side, he could touch the other hole with his longest finger. For some reason, that amused him.

"Haven! Are you saying my brother is alive?"

"He was when I left." But the memory of Pierce's ashen face made him blanch, his own pain suddenly fading a bit. Pierce was still in the well, probably in shock, possibly still bleeding. He eyed Fuller, who still hadn't moved. "We need to get help. Do you have your phone?"

It was almost comical the way Jordan's eyes widened in surprise. "I can't believe I didn't think of that." He pulled it from his back pocket and hit the button. Then hit it again, and again. "Shit! It's dead! How can it be dead?"

For some reason, Haven wasn't surprised. "She didn't say 'ant' at all. She said 'Sergeant.'"

"What are you talking about?"

"That's why the batteries are dead."

"Haven, you're not making any sense. It's freaking me out. I need you to stay with me."

Haven shook his head, trying to refocus. He found himself staring at Fuller. "Find his car keys. We can use the radio in his car."

"Good idea. Can you hold the gun?"

Haven could only blink at him. "I think so." The world was starting to go a bit blurry. He was beginning to shiver. "Jesus, it's freezing in here."

"Shit! Hang in there, Haven."

"I'm fine."

"Can you walk? Can you go down to the car?"

Haven tried to stand, but discovered the pain he'd felt before had only been a teaser. This time, he really did scream. He found himself crouched on the floor, gasping for air.

"Not good," Jordan said.

Chief Fuller stirred with a groan, putting a hand to his head.

Whatever advantage they'd had was quickly running out.

"Go!" Haven said. "Break the window in his car. Call for help."

"But he's waking up!"

"Don't worry about me. You need to get help for Pierce."

"Haven—"

There was a moment when nothing could be said. Jordan had to make a choice, and Haven knew there was only one way it could go. He couldn't even blame Jordan for choosing his brother first and leaving Haven alone with a killer.

And then, like some kind of miracle, Haven heard sirens.

"Am I dreaming that?" Haven asked, looking up at Jordan. "Is it normal to hear sirens when you die?"

Jordan tilted his head, listening. A second later, he laughed with delight. The relief on his face was unmistakable. "You're not dreaming," he said, just as the strobes of red and blue began flashing through the nearest window. "I don't know how, but it seems the cavalry has arrived."

Three Months Later

The construction was coming along nicely.

The bones of the house remained the same, but everything else about it was new. New porch, new paint, new floor plan. New carpet, new furniture…

New owner.

"I can't believe you bought it," Jordan said, as Pierce and Haven led him across the recently mown front lawn and up the steps. The house now sported a broad, wrap-around porch and a polished oak front door with sparkling panes of beveled glass.

The windows would never be boarded up again.

They stepped inside and stopped in the entryway. Jordan eyed the staircase, which had also been redesigned and rebuilt. The horrible chandelier had been removed. Skylights and broad, two-story windows offered better light anyway.

"It looks good," Jordan conceded. "But why in the world would you want to live here?"

Haven couldn't explain it. Not exactly. But it all went back to that night.

The night he'd gone down the well.

Haven had clung to the ladder, his cell phone in his hand, until the moment the gun went off.

Jordan and Pierce both told him Chief Fuller had aimed at the left side of Pierce's chest. The barrel of the gun had been only inches away from Pierce's heart.

So how had the bullet hit him in the right shoulder instead?

"Something pushed me," Pierce had told Haven in the hospital. "I saw the gun come up, and then it was like somebody shoved me hard in the chest. It had to be Elise. That's why our cell phone batteries were dead. She drained them in order to save me."

Jordan chose to believe Pierce had flinched away at exactly the right moment.

Haven wasn't so sure.

The fact that Jordan had suddenly become the skeptic and Haven and Pierce the believers wasn't lost on anyone.

Down in the well, Haven's call to Linsey had gone through. She'd answered, and said "Hello?" twice. He hadn't said anything for fear Chief Fuller would hear him, but Linsey swore she heard five distinct words before the line went dead.

Send help to the well.

Linsey had followed through.

"Was it my voice?" Haven asked, when they talked on the phone the next morning. "Did it sound like me?"

Linsey said no, it sounded like a woman.

Haven didn't have the heart to ask her if it had sounded like her dead sister. She was busy enough dealing with a newborn. No need to freak her out any more than necessary.

Pierce had been unconscious but still breathing when the paramedics found him. Once he was out of the well, it hadn't taken them long to get him stabilized. The doctors had removed the bullet from his shoulder, wrapped his twisted ankle, and assured everyone he'd make a full recovery.

And he had.

Haven's wound had been mostly superficial. They'd taped him up, given him antibiotics and a few painkillers, and sent him home. He'd sort of hoped he'd at least have a wicked scar when it was all said and done.

But he didn't.

Chief Fuller had suffered a concussion from Haven's blow with the flashlight, but that was the least of his problems. A search of his hunting cabin turned up a mountain of evidence, including photos and videos of the torture, rape, and murder of each woman he'd abducted. There was no pattern. No neat explanation. Even the five-year time frame estimated by the original coroner hadn't been exactly correct. Each girl had simply been in the wrong place at the wrong time. Each had seen a police officer and assumed he was trustworthy. Each one had spent at least one terrible day regretting her decision.

Haven tried not to dwell on the horror of Elise's final hours. He took comfort in knowing she'd fought until the very end.

The good news was that between Fuller's lurid trophies and Jordan's recording, there was no chance of the man going free. He was facing eight counts of murder—Cassie Kennedy, Joseph Gustafson, the three original bodies from the well, Elise, and the two other women found with her. There were a slew of other charges pending, but the short version was, he'd spend the rest of his life in a concrete cell.

Craig had promptly resigned from the police department and moved to Montana. He'd also deleted his Facebook account.

But that wasn't the end of the story.

It wasn't until a week later, when Pierce and Haven were lying together in bed, that Pierce admitted the rest.

"She talked to me."

They'd grown accustomed to Haven's hotel room by that point, although Haven had already begun thinking about moving back to Hobbsburg. Somehow, he felt it was where he was always meant to be.

He hadn't had the nerve yet to ask Pierce what his long-term plans were.

"Who talked to you?" Haven asked.

"Elise."

Haven sat up and turned to face him, his heart suddenly light and his fingers trembling. "When was this?"

"When I was down the well."

Haven's mouth went dry. He didn't want to believe.

Then again, maybe he did.

"What did she say?"

"She said, 'Hang on. He'll fix it.' And when I said, 'Who?' she said, 'Nothing scares Haven.' Then she stayed with me until the paramedics arrived."

"That doesn't make any sense at all. She was always trying to scare me."

Pierce laughed before taking his hand and pulling him back down into bed.

Into his arms.

"'Trying' being the key word there. She never succeeded."

Haven lay there, contemplating the possibilities. He'd never believed in ghosts. Besides, Pierce had been unconscious and in shock when the paramedics found him. He'd also lost an alarming amount of blood. Had Elise really been there or had it merely been a near-death experience? Haven would probably never know, just like he'd never know if it had been Cassie speaking to them twelve years ago during their séance or only Elise playing one of her elaborate pranks.

Even when you experience something first hand, you're left with more questions than answers and no proof whatsoever.

"I assume you rewired the whole damn place?" Jordan asked, bringing Haven back to the present.

"Obviously," Pierce said.

Jordan's gaze shifted toward Haven. "And you filled in the well, right?"

"Oh, God yes. That was the first thing I did." He thought he might rebuild the aboveground structure though, just as it had once been—a perfect stone ring with a little roof and bucket hanging from a chain. It wouldn't be functional, but it'd be pretty and innocent, somehow symbolizing youth and life and the fact that wishes sometimes came true. He pictured it surrounded by rose bushes, like a shrine. But, for now, he was happy just to have that dark tunnel into the Earth gone.

"You want to see upstairs?" Pierce asked his brother.

Jordan eyed the landing at the top of the stairs—the place where he'd almost been forced to put a noose around his own neck. "Maybe another day."

"Suit yourself. I want to make sure they installed the skylight in the master bedroom right." Pierce was already halfway up the stairs. "I don't want it leaking on Haven during a storm."

Jordan and Haven stayed by the front door, watching until he'd disappeared into the bedroom. It was the first time they'd been alone together since the incident.

"That's cute," Jordan said, "the way he pretends he won't be here to fix it for you."

Haven ducked his head, for some reason wanting to hide how happy those words made him. He and Pierce hadn't quite spelled out the details of their relationship yet. Not in words, at any rate. But it was true Pierce seemed keenly invested in helping with the house, making sure the wiring was all up to code, offering suggestions, even urging Haven to expand the master bedroom into the neighboring room they'd once shared. "I hope he will be."

"Are you kidding? He was already crazy about you. Then you had to go and save his life. You'll never get rid of him now."

"Uh…well…"

Jordan turned then, meeting Haven's eyes with an intensity that sent him back a step. Jordan, who loved his brother so much, it seemed he couldn't help but love the person he thought had saved him. "Maybe you shouldn't cut him loose after all."

Having Jordan's approval made Haven's chest feel light as air. It made the sunshine outside seem brighter than before. "I never planned to anyway."

Jordan sighed, his intensity giving way to grudging laughter. "Fair enough." Jordan turned away to watch up the stairs for his brother. "You saved us. I think about it every goddamned day, but I never even said thank you."

Haven shrugged, uncomfortable with Jordan's gratitude. He didn't feel like a hero. "I didn't really do anything." He'd only done the next logical thing, and the next, and the next.

The rest had been luck. Or timing. Or maybe ghosts.

It was hard to say.

"You never answered my question," Jordan said, leaning his elbow on the brand-new stair railing. The smile he gave Haven made him look alarmingly like his brother. "There are tons of houses in Hobbsburg. Why in the world would you want this one?"

"Because…"

After Pierce had told him about his time in the well—about talking to Elise—Haven had lain there the rest of the night, wondering what to believe. He'd never found an answer, but when the sun came up the next morning, he'd made arrangements to enter the Gustafson house again—legally this time. He'd walked through the sad, dilapidated building with the stunned real estate agent, seeing it with new eyes.

And when he stepped off the back porch and looked toward the woods, he could have sworn he saw his cousin disappearing into the trees.

"For Elise," he said at last. "I bought it for Elise."

And whether the sound he heard as he lay in bed at night was his cousin's laughter as she ran from the purple worbles, or only the wind whistling through a poorly installed skylight…

Haven was happy either way.

ABOUT THE AUTHOR

Marie Sexton lives in Colorado. She's a fan of just about anything that involves muscular young men piling on top of each other. In particular, she loves the Denver Broncos and enjoys going to the games with her husband. Her imaginary friends often tag along. Marie has one daughter, two cats, and one dog, all of whom seem bent on destroying what remains of her sanity. She loves them anyway.

Website and Blog:
http://mariesexton.net/

Facebook:
http://www.facebook.com/MarieSexton.author/

Twitter:
https://twitter.com/MarieSexton

Email: msexton.author@gmail.com

ALSO BY MARIE SEXTON

Promises
A to Z
The Letter Z
Strawberries for Dessert
Paris A to Z
Fear, Hope, and Bread Pudding
Between Sinners and Saints
Song of Oestend
Saviours of Oestend
Blind Space
Second Hand
Never a Hero
Family Man
Flowers for Him
One More Soldier
Cinder
Normal Enough
Roped In
Chapter 5 and the Axe-Wielding Maniac
Apartment 14 and the Devil Next Door
Lost Along the Way
Shotgun
Winter Oranges
Damned If You Do
Trailer Trash
Making Waves

50874390R00125

Made in the USA
Middletown, DE
05 November 2017